Death Calls The Dean

A Cotton Cunningham Academic Mystery

Dennis Collins

NFB Publishing
Buffalo, New York

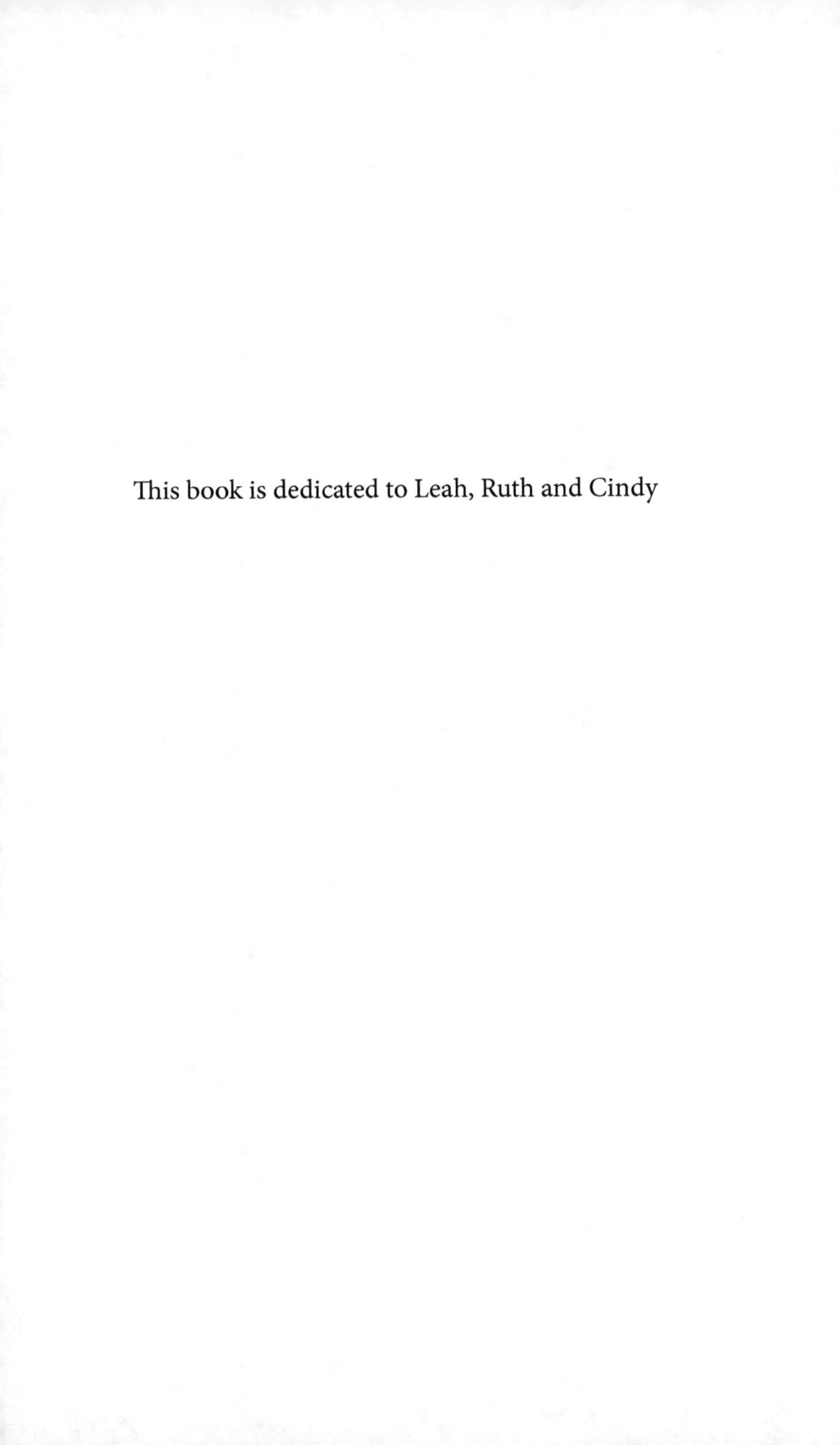

This book is dedicated to Leah, Ruth and Cindy

Death Calls the Dean

Chapter 1

January 22, 1948
The University of Buffalo
9:00 PM

"Who the hell does she think I am?"

Chaz Barker, a PhD student in Political Science at the University of Buffalo, asked himself that question as he sauntered across the UB campus. A light snow was buffeted by a strong lake effect wind drifting in off Lake Erie. The salted sidewalks sparkled in the glare of the Victorian streetlights. The early winter was a portent of more calamitous weather to come. The holiday break had come to an end and students were moving back into the dorms. A campus that had lain dark for the better part of a month was now bustling with the sounds of students and parents hauling boxes and suitcases up stairwells.

Barker had stayed in Buffalo during the break to polish up his doctoral work. This semester would be for fine tuning his thesis and preparing for his orals. It was Thursday night and he had just left Lockwood Library after a lackluster night of research. He was still angry over a meeting with his thesis advisor, Jill Asbury, the day before. Dr Asbury was a young, up and coming professor in the Political Science Department. When examining his research project, the week before, she suggested that they could co-author an extension of some of his ideas after he had been granted a doctorate. When Chaz objected, she became quite cold and remote. Then, just yesterday, when she had been called out of her office during a discussion with Chaz, he noticed a file balanced on a windowsill with a familiar title.

The Effects of Insider Trading Information on the Political Conscience

Chaz jumped out of his chair. That was precisely the angle that he was developing in his PhD research. She was stealing his ideas!

And they were good ideas. His father, Jenson Barker, was a professor emeritus in the Economics Department of Kenyon College in Ohio. Together, they had developed the thesis idea with hopes that his eventual doctoral publication would turn into a book. There was no way he would let her get away with such thievery.

With file in hand, he confronted her outright when she returned to her office.

"Professor Asbury, this is my intellectual property. I can't believe that you've stolen it from me!"

Red in the face, she went on the offensive.

"What are you doing, Barker, rummaging through my private papers!"

Suffice to say, the meeting ended with Barker storming out of the office, with threats to take it to a higher level.

Evidence of plagiarism was not all that Barker had on her. A few weeks before, when he had showed up at her office unannounced, he had been greeted by moans and groans emanating from within. It was late in the day, after the secretary had left. Not embarrassed in the least, he had taken a seat in a faraway corner. Some fifteen minutes later, a dark haired, blue-eyed co-ed slipped out of the office

door. Tall and athletic, she moved with an air of authority. She was dressed professionally, with a white cotton
sweater and red pleated skirt. As she walked through the
outer office, their eyed locked. Strangely enough, Barker
thought, she had no look of embarrassment or shame. In
fact, her features were caught up in anger and defiance.

Barker was surprised. To be caught, in flagrante delic-
to, a lesbian relationship no less, was an offense that could
put both student and teacher in a tenuous position.

After she left, Chaz stood in the hallway by a window
that looked out over the courtyard below. As the young
woman left the building, she was joined by two figures.
The first one was tall with wind swept blond hair and a
slight limp. He was dressed in a pea coat and blue jeans.
The other was short, barrel chested and nervously scan-
ning the courtyard. As they walked away, funnels of snow
whipped up all around them as they whispered conspira-
torially.

Barker, repulsed by the whole scene, quickly left the
building by a side stairwell.

If he would have stayed a minute longer, he would
have witnessed another figure, approach Asbury's office.

As he walked across campus that Thursday night, Chaz
thought that he had enough evidence to ensure that the
professor would never be a threat to his publishing future.

Turning the corner of the bus garage that led to the
student parking lot, he never saw the 2X4 that arched
through the air and crashed into his head. A jarring pain
enveloped his consciousness, and his final feeling was a
mixture of snow and blood in his mouth. It was the last
anyone ever saw of Chaz Barker alive.

Chapter 2

October 11, 1968
The University of Buffalo

The construction crew was working on a deadline. They were building storage sheds for a government project. The University had submitted a proposal to establish a laboratory that dealt with thermal stress, exercise, altered gravity and hypobaric environments. Supported by the Department of Defense, it had attracted a certain amount of protest from student activists. The proposal was named Project Themis after the Greek goddess of divine law and order.

The workers were operating on a staggered lunch schedule and a group was eating at a picnic table under one of the few shade trees that occupied that portion of the Main Street campus. They were discussing what they were going to do that Friday evening. Jed Kowalski, a Pole from South Buffalo was holding court.

"Me and the Mrs. are going to take in a fish fry at St. Agnes tonight. After that, maybe find a place to dance. We got a babysitter for the kids, and it's been a while."

A few others mentioned similar plans. They were finishing up when an out of breath worker ran up to the group.

"Hey guys, we dug up something and it looks like it's been there a long time.!"

A couple of hours later, Jefferson Drew, head of campus security, was standing over the excavation, with his hands on his hips and a scowl on his face. He had two calls to make. The first one was to University President Martin Meyerson and the second was to history professor Cotton Cunningham.

"THERE was no wallet on the body. We figured whoever killed him took it to prevent identification. What they neglected to do was remove his college ring – graduating class of 1946 at UB. We're having the Buffalo Police check their missing person's files from that year on," said Drew.

Jefferson Drew was short and slim, dressed in a security uniform that was neatly pressed and regulation down to the last detail. He hair was crew cut and his shoes were spit shined.

He was in the office of UB President Martin Meyerson. Also present was History professor Cotton Cunningham, who was Meyerson's representative to the student body. He was a major player in the investigation of a murder that had occurred the year before. Cunningham was tall and lanky, a shade over six feet. He wore his dark hair longer now that he was no longer with the Buffalo police. He was dressed casually in khaki pants with a button-down white shirt and dark blue crew sweater.

"It might be interesting to ask some of the teaching staff that were here post World War 2, if they knew of any students who had disappeared suddenly, "said Cunningham.

"After last year, we don't need any more incidents," said Meyerson.

Meyerson was sitting behind a well-polished desk situated in front of a bay window that overlooked a campus swarming with students making their way to and from classes. It was one of those warm autumn days that made the fallen leaves seem out of place. Meyerson was dressed in a conservative blue suit, blue tie, stripped shirt and paisley tie. By mid-day, he would have probably discarded the suit and rolled up his sleeves.

Meyerson was referring to a spate of incidents that had included a murder, a bombing and an assassination attempt on Mohammad Ali who was visiting the campus as a speaker. It had culminated in the culprit being hurled over the rapids below the Niagara Falls.

Meyerson was sympathetic to any victims, but he was also aware of the ramifications such incidents could have from a public relations standpoint. His phone would burn up with calls from disenchanted alumni and parents of perspective students.

"Once we have a possible identification, the Buffalo Police can use dental records to make a positive match," said Drew.

The phone rang and Meyerson picked it up. There was a pause as he listened to the voice at the other end. He pulled over a pad and started writing.

"All right, please get me the paperwork as soon as possible."

He glanced up at Cunningham and Drew with a grim look.

"After looking through their missing person files, the police found a likely match. Chaz Barker, a doctoral student in Political Science, disappeared in January of 1948. He was never located. The police are trying to contact next of kin in Ohio to get medical records. His parents are dead but there's a brother who lives in Ohio," said Meyerson.

"I had experience with buried bodies when I worked with the police, but they were usually mob related killings," said Cunningham.

Cunningham was a former Buffalo Police detective who had taken a disability leave to study History at the University. He received a PhD and was hired full time. Meyerson convinced him to be his representative to the student body. He was well liked by students and his presence came in handy during the politically charged times that the University was facing.

"I'll continue working with the police on the identification process and see if I can nail down more information about the student," said Drew.

"I'll talk to some professors I know who are in the Political Science and History departments and might have remembered him," said Cunningham.

Meyerson nodded. "Get back to me as soon as possible. I want to stay ahead of this. I'll be getting phone calls from parents who will want to know about this incident and how safe the campus is."

Chapter 3

Norton Union was a mess. The usual lunchtime rush of students had left their debris all over tables and the floor. The custodial staff was bustling around trying to clean up, but they were severely understaffed. It smelled of pizza, baloney and sweat.

Cotton was sitting at a clean table and across from him was Cassandra Day. She was an academic blueblood who seemed to be part of everything important that had transpired on the UB campus for the previous thirty years. She was a professor emeritus who started her career as a graduate student in the New School of Social Research in the 1920's. She studied with such notables as Charles Beard, John Dewey, and Thorstein Veblen. These pioneers broke away from Columbia University during the post WWI years. They envisioned a new type of educational environment with closer ties to European Institutions of higher learning. It was an outgrowth of the Progressive movement in American society.

Cassandra thrived in the New School atmosphere and fell in love with one of its leaders, Joshua Day. They married in 1926 and both found jobs at the University of Buffalo in mid 1930. Joshua Day died of Cancer in 1942. Cassandra continued in the history department until her retirement in 1962. She kept an office and taught an occasional graduate course, one of which Cotton had taken.

She continued in her early eighties to be a firebrand in the classroom. She and Cotton had developed a friendship and stayed in touch through faculty dinners and fundraisers.

She accepted Cotton's invitation to lunch, but when she glided into the student union, he realized that he would have been better off asking her to dine at the Cloister, Park Lane or the Rue Franklin. The epitome of haute couture, Day managed to bridge the gap between post WWII fashion and the emerging sixties styles. She wore tweed bell bottoms with a stylish wide metal belt and a sleeveless sweater over a white silk blouse. Her pearls shone brightly and at least a half dozen rings adorned her fingers. Although she dressed high society, she never flaunted it. She had a raspy voice, the result of too much smoking in her earlier years.

"Cotton, dear, so glad to see you again. It's been what,since the symposium on capitalism last semester. The one where Gabriel reigned supreme?"

Gabriel Kolko was a revisionist historian who had made a name for himself in the early sixties with the publication of two books – *The Triumph of Conservatism and Railroads and Regulation 1877-1916.* In these books he disputed the widely held thesis that government regulated business. Instead, he postulated the exact opposite – the business regulated the government.

Kolko had a devout following, especially among young scholars. He was recruited by the University and was the young Turk of the history department. Cassandra was an admirer.

"He certainly rose quickly," said Cotton. "He's popular with the students because of his opposition to the Viet

Nam War. He's so disappointed in the government that I think he's looking for a position outside the country. I hear that York University in Toronto is wooing him."

"What a loss for UB if he leaves," moaned Day.

Cotton steered the conversation in another direction. "I'm sure you've heard about the body found on campus?"

"I've read about it in the papers, but I'm not sure of the particulars."

"The police identified him by his class ring. His name was Chaz Barker, class of 1946. He was working on a doctorate in Political Science. Marty Meyerson has asked me to check with some professors who were on the faculty back then to see if any of them recall his name."

"I was History, of course, but we were close to the Political Science department. We were on the same wing. I can't place the name, but I seem to remember the disappearance of a student around that time. You would be better of checking with Dean Asbury. I believe she was a young untenured professor in the Political Science department back then. She would know more about it."

Dean Asbury was the Dean of Humanities. In her late forties, she had assumed that position upon the death of Sandy Lawson two years previous. In Cotton's opinion, she was an opportunist, skilled in departmental backstabbing.

"I'll do that," said Cotton. "Can you think of any others who might be helpful?"

"Randy McPherson was around back then, but he was in Sociology. Dolores Davis was in Sociology also and both still teaching. They're your best bet.

"Great," said Cotton. They spent the next half hour discussing curriculum revisions and the state of student activism.

"It's good to see students concerned with the situation on campus. I remember back in my graduate days in New York City during the 1920s, I was considered a radical. Many of us flirted with the Communist Party. It was just after the Russian Revolution and the idea of people wrestling power from a politically corrupt system was intoxicating. Later, when Stalin took over, and we learned of the atrocities, we came to realize that regardless of the system, if the leaders were totalitarian, then people would suffer."

After parting ways with Day, Cotton strolled across campus to his office in Diefendorf Hall. Due to a spate of warm weather, the campus was redolent of a tropical setting. A casual carpet of leaves blew gently across the urban scene. Students were taking advantage of the summer- like weather by lounging around benches with friends and lovers. A football was being thrown about and music was spilling out of a dormitory window. Was it the Young Rascals? Of course, *People got to be Free.*

Chapter 4

Cotton knew Randy McPherson professionally, having served on several interdisciplinary committees with him. He was short and wiry, a viciously competitive handball player and a dedicated bird watcher. He was old school in his dress – corduroy jackets with elbow patches and the obligatory pipe. A former Marine who had served in both world wars, he was known to be tough on his students, peppering them with questions with a cadence that would make a drill sergeant proud. His office was neatly laid out – books in rows arranged by height, piles of papers squared away. He was cordial, but Cotton got the feeling he was anxious to get back to ravaging term papers with his red pen.

"Damn well can't open my windows on a beautiful day because of all the bullshit music these kids like to play. What did you say the students name was? Barker? And his first name was Chaz? What the hell kind of name is that?"

He was rummaging through his desk drawers. "What year did you say?"

McPherson's grade books went back to the 1920s

"He was a political science major, so you might not have had him and anyways his grades won't tell me much," said Cotton. "What I'm really interested in is whether you remember a student that went missing back in 1948."

McPherson stroked his chin. "Come to think of it, I do recall that incident. I remember because the police came through and interviewed most of the teachers in the humanities. I couldn't tell them much because I didn't have him in any of my classes. I think he was a graduate student in the Political Science department."

"That's right, Dr. McPherson, "said Cotton. "He hadn't finished his thesis or taken his orals yet. According to the police reports and newspaper articles, he was last seen on a Thursday evening at Lockwood Library."

"I don't mix much with the Political Science people," said McPherson. "I find them a bit condescending. They were an old bunch back then, right after the war, set in their ways. I remember they gave that young teacher a lot of flak when she was up for tenure."

"Who would that be?" asked Cotton.

"Let me think... Sanderson? No, she was only here for a couple of years before she up and got married and moved... Yardley? No, she wasn't even in Political Science. Christ, Cunningham, why don't you get your ass down to the library and check out the yearbooks for those years!"

As he walked out of McPherson's office, Cotton wondered why he hadn't thought of that himself.

A student in ragged bellbottoms and a tee-shirt that proclaimed *make love not war*, directed him to a wall of yearbooks. He took down the books from 1946 though 1948. He first searched for Barker in what would have been his graduation year. He found him easy enough, dressed in a pinstriped suit, looking somber with a bowl haircut and a pencil thin mustache. Underneath the picture were words, "Failure is not an option," and "Economics is my baby."

Cotton did a cursory examination of various clubs and organizations to find Barker, but without success. It seemed like Barker wasn't into anything other than his studies.

His next task was to visit the faculty pages, especially in Political Science. He didn't find anyone he knew until 1948. There was McPherson's mystery woman, and she was very familiar to Cotton. Swept up hair with black rimmed glasses and sharp features. A very young Jill Asbury stared back at him. In 1948, she was an untenured professor. In 1968, she was Dr. Jillian Asbury, Dean of Humanities.

A phone call to the Dean's secretary was a dead end. She was out of town at a conference and wouldn't be back until the end of the week. He decided to return to his office and prepare for his evening class. As he walked through campus, he wondered about Barker's death. He worked some cold cases when he was a homicide detective with the Buffalo Police Department. They were difficult for many reasons. People's' memories faded after years gone by. Crime scenes change-a house could be torn down or an apartment building renovated. In the case of Chaz Barker, the crime scene was unknown. It would take leg work to reconstruct his death and he had classes to teach, papers to grade and committees to serve on. He also had a relationship to maintain and that reminded him of a dinner date he had to keep.

Chapter 5

Jen Valley was a professor of history at UB. She was involved in a murder investigation the previous year. Unknown to her, Valley was dating the murderer at the time. He assaulted her and her injuries led to an extended hospital stay. Visits from Cotton every day helped her in her convalescence. They grew close and were now dating.

Jen was a vivacious blonde, small in stature, with piercing blue eyes, and a flashing smile. She was dressed casually in denim bell bottoms and a frilly white blouse.

"If I had known you were taking me to such a swanky place, I would have dressed for the occasion," said Valley. They were seated at the Your Host restaurant on Delaware Avenue.

"I thought a little comfort food would be in order," said Cotton with a grin.

Your Host was the common man's restaurant that had locations all over Western New York. They were open 24 hours a day and offered a bottomless cup of coffee. It was a great place to go after a night of drinking. You could eat at the long counter or at lime green seats that flanked booths on the opposite wall. It wasn't fancy, but it was clean, and the service was friendly.

Cotton ordered the New York strip steak and Jen the ham steak with pineapple. They caught up on campus gossip while waiting for their food.

"Tomorrow is my longest teaching day and now Jack scheduled a faculty meeting at the end of the afternoon," she said.

Jack Larson was the history chair. He loathed the position and tried to funnel as much responsibility to untenured professors as possible. Jen was already on three committees and had a heavy teaching load. On top of that she was working on more than one article for publication. Advisor to numerous campus clubs, she had close ties to her students and was well like by her peers.

Cotton had the same teaching load and publishing responsibilities, but less committee work due to his ex officio role as an advisor to President Meyerson. At a time when campus unrest and political tensions were high, he was invaluable because of his experience as a homicide detective in the Buffalo Police Department and because of his close relationship with many Buffalo politicians.

"I take it that the President has asked you to consult on the body that was unearthed last week," she said while delicately cutting into her ham steak.

"Yes, and before you go any further, there is nothing to discuss other than what you read in the papers. I've talked with some faculty that were on campus when the student matriculated, but they have little recollection of the incident. My next step is to find out who his advisors was and hope that he or she is in the area."

There was a considerable age difference between the two, but they shared the same teaching field. Cotton was more of an outdoor type, favoring long hikes, bicycles, and ski trips, while Jen was more in tune with concerts, both classical and folk, and was a frequent visitor to the Albright Knox Art Gallery. Generally, they complimented and tried to support each other. The thought of moving in together had been on Cotton's mind, although he hadn't brought it up to Valley.

Cotton lived in a small two bedroom walk up off Delaware Avenue. Jen had a smaller apartment over an antique shop in the Allentown section of Buffalo. They both enjoyed their own space and Cotton wondered whether cohabitation would put a cramp in their relationship.

After finishing their meal, they decided on a short stroll down Delaware Avenue, peeking into various shops. It was a pleasant night with a slight wind. A sudden chill made them appreciate the last vestiges of a fading sun. They ended up at Cotton's apartment for a glass of wine and nodded off on the couch to Eyewitness News with Irv Weinstein.

Chapter 6

The following day, Cotton spoke with Jefferson Drew over the phone.

"We have a medical examiner's report. Even though the body was decomposed, the skull was intact, and he found an indentation that he estimated had been caused by a blunt object. He narrowed it down a bit. He said it wasn't a baseball bat because it wasn't rounded. Not a wrench either. He thinks it might have been a piece of wood, maybe a sharp end of a 2X4.

"Whatever it was, it was a violent death," said Cotton.

"Yes, it was, "said Drew. "It was murder."

Dean Jillian Asbury was staying at the Ritz Carlton in Boston, one of the perks of being an administrator of a prestigious eastern university. It was evening and she had just settled in with a glass of wine when the phone rang. The voice on the other end of the line began with no introduction.

"They found the body."

Asbury froze. Her mind raced back twenty years.

"Where?" Asbury blurted out.

Her whole body was shaking. The glass of wine fell to the floor and splattered on the nearby wall.

"Where it was put to get us out of the fucking mess you put us in," the voice said.

"Do they know who it is?" Asbury said.

"I never expected them to dig it up. It's that damn Themis Project. Oh, they'll eventually figure out who it is."

"What will we do?" croaked Asbury.

"You will do nothing. You will continue as if nothing happened. You answer questions with a clear head. You are an innocent academic with little information to offer. Yes, you were his academic advisor. They will find that out by checking the records. That means nothing."

"I don't think I can do this," Asbury said.

"You don't have a choice," said the voice. "You're a whore in more ways than one."

The phone line went dead.

Asbury buried her head in her hands.

Chapter 7

Dolores Davis sat behind her desk in her campus office opposite Cotton Cunningham. There were pictures of her with prominent politicians on the walls. They spanned the years from the thirties all the way to the late fifties. She had been an advisor to many of them on both the city, state, and even national levels. Her field was political campaigning and she had conducted many. She stood nearly six feet in heels and was an intimidating presence when she ushered Cotton into her office.

She was severely dressed in a grey blouse with her hair pulled back into a bun. Her eyes were dark and recessed and the skin on her face appeared drawn and colorless. Cotton had seen corpses with more life.

"Professor Cunningham, I'm at a loss as to why you are here."

Cotton got right to the point. "Dr. Davis, are you aware of the body that was dug up on campus?"

"I am and I don't see why a faculty member should be interrogating me about it. On whose authority are you here?"

Cotton explained to her his role in the investigation and how his authority stemmed from the President.

"I still don't see my connection to that matter." she said.

"We are interviewing faculty who were teaching in the

years after the war in the hopes of gathering information about the student."

"You realize that by pointing out that era, you are aging me considerably. That's not very flattering to a woman."

"I'm wondering whether you might have known the student. His name was Chaz Barker. Do you recall his disappearance?"

Davis eyes rolled and she laughed – more like a cough than an expression of humor.

"You seriously expect me to remember a student from twenty years ago?" she asked.

"Perhaps not a student, but the incident must have been memorable," Cotton remarked.

"I do remember a police investigation on campus during the late forties, but I wasn't involved. What was his major?"

"Political Science," said Cotton.

"My field is Sociology; I doubt that our paths crossed," she said.

Cotton could feel a rising tide of antagonism directed at him.

"Perhaps you might be familiar with some other faculty from that period. Dean Asbury was just beginning her career then," said Cotton.

"Of course, I am familiar with Dean Asbury, more so when she ascended to her position as dean than in her earlier years," she said.

"She's out of town now, But I'll be getting in touch with her when she returns," said Cotton. "Thank you for your time. If anything occurs to you in the future, please let me know."

She stared at him with no expression, and he took that as his dismissal.

Chapter 8

A few days later, he contacted Dean Asbury's secretary to set up a date to speak.

The secretary returned to the phone almost immediately. "The dean would like to speak to you."

After a short pause a husky voice came on the line.

"Professor Cunningham, what do you need to see me for?" Her tone was confrontational.

"Dean Asbury, thank you for your time. President Meyerson has asked me to investigate the death of a student from twenty years ago, whose body was just discovered on campus. He was a Political Science major. We thought that since you were a member of that department in 1948, you might have remembered him."

"I have no idea what you are talking about, Cunningham. I have been out of town for almost a week and work is piled up on my desk and now this from ages ago."

She was shouting into the phone by then.

"How dare you connect me to such a sordid affair!"

Cotton was completely caught off guard by her outburst and before he could respond she had hung up.

"What was that all about he wondered?" He could chalk up Dolores Davis as just a contrary personality, but Asbury's response was very unusual. He needed to speak to her in person, but he needed help from higher up.

"SHE shouted at you over the phone?" asked Marty Meyerson.

"That's right. I just mentioned the student's death and she went on a rampage," said Cotton.

"Why did you ask to interview her? Do you know of any connection between her and Barker?" asked Meyerson.

"I know she was an untenured professor in the Political Science department back then. It's not unlikely that she would know him. I never got far enough in our conversation to find out. She hung up on me," said Cotton.

"That's strange," said Meyerson. "I'll give her a call and straighten this all out."

Chapter 9

Cotton was in his office the next day when his phone rang.

"This is Dean Asbury's office. She would like you to drop by and see her this afternoon. What time would be convenient for you?"

They arranged a 4:00 appointment after Cotton's early afternoon class.

The class dealing with the Reconstruction period, was very lively. Some of the students stayed after class to talk about the presence of project Themis on campus.

"I don't think that a project linked to the Department of Defense should be allowed on campus," said Jake LaPorte, a senior from Long Island.

"How about ROTC?" asked Cotton.

"A college is of place for learning," said Martina O'Brian, a junior from Niagara Falls. "We shouldn't be training people to kill."

"What do you think Dr. Cunningham?" asked Jake.

"I'm coming from a different perspective that you are," said Cotton. "I fought in the Korean War, where the United States was a part of a United Nations Peace Keeping Force. I believe what we did then was justified, but when MacArthur wanted to use the atomic bomb against the Chinese, I was completely opposed. I do believe that ROTC has a place on campus. Young men and women want to get a college education and then pursue their careers in the military."

The conversation was a healthy one. Cotton believed in a constructive dialogue in the classroom and often scrapped a perfectly good lesson plan to let the students have their say. Today, the students were carrying on the discussion out in the hall while Cotton was packing his briefcase. He had just enough time to drop off his belongings in his office before heading off to his appointment with Asbury.

On his way to the administrative offices, Cotton passed a young couple making out on a park bench. They were oblivious to their surroundings and quite amorous in their intent. Cotton remembered similar scenes from his youth, when a bottle of Boone's Farm and a willing girl could lead to a day to remember.

A cold autumn wind had picked up, scurrying leaves and debris across campus. An overcast sky hid whatever sun was left in the day. Frisbees and footballs were being tossed around and a ponytailed student in a denim jacket and jeans was strumming a guitar to a Dylan tune – something from Highway 51 Revisited – *You don't need a weatherman to know which way the wind blows.*

Cotton didn't have to wait long. He found Asbury and her secretary conversing in the outer office. When the Dean saw Cotton, she quickly came over, shook hands, and ushered him into her office and shut the door.

"Dr. Cunningham, I would like to apologize for my behavior on the phone yesterday. I have been under quite a bit of pressure the last few weeks dealing with college business and personal matters. There was no reason to take it out on you. Please sit down and ask any questions.

Anything I can do to solve the mystery of what happened to that poor soul, I am more than willing."

"Dean, the student in question, Chaz Barker was a political science major during his time at UB. In 1948, he was working on his PhD thesis. In January of that year, he disappeared and was never seen again until his body was recently discovered by construction workers who were digging a foundation for a storage shed to be used by Project Themis. What I would like to know is whether you knew Chaz."

Asbury tented her fingers before she replied.

"As a matter of fact, I did. I was his faculty advisor on his PhD thesis."

Cotton was momentarily taken aback. For days, he had been getting no traction in this investigation and now he was presented with a substantial lead.

"Can you remember the last time you saw him alive?" he asked.

Asbury frowned and was silent for a moment, as if thinking was a painful process,

"I believe it was our last meeting about his thesis. I can't be completely accurate about that. I might have passed him on campus in the days that followed. The only reason that I remembered the meeting was that I was asked the question by the police after his disappearance."

Cotton settled back in his seat. They occupied a leather coach on one side of the large office. Bookshelves lined the opposite wall. A huge antique desk stood in a bay window opposite the office door. The desk was meticulously neat. There was a lectern with a large library edition of Webster's dictionary sitting on it. A Royal typewriter sat on the other side of the desk. The bay window held a variety of plants including a Wandering Jew and a Philodendron. Pictures lined the wall over the coach depicting her world travels.

"What kind of student was Chaz Barker?" asked Cotton.

Again, a pause. Her hands were clenched.

"Very good as an undergraduate. He was highly inquisitive and very imaginative. He had an excellent topic for his PhD thesis. It had to do with both economics and political science."

"Do you remember the exact topic?" Cotton asked.

"Something to do with voting rights and the economy. It was twenty years ago, and I never got a copy of the thesis. "

"At the last meeting, how was his demeanor? Was he depressed, happy, stressed out?" asked Cotton.

"Again, a long time ago, but I think I would have noticed any serious moods," she said.

"And after he disappeared, what did you think?" asked Cotton.

"I remembered wondering why a successful student with a bright future ahead of him would just leave town without giving notice to someone."

'So, there was no indication of any problems either with other students or teachers?" Cotton asked.

"No," said Asbury. "I can't say if he had many friends, but his relationship with me was cordial."

Cotton left her office without a distinct feeling about Asbury. He did notice one thing. During the last few minutes of the interview, Dean Asbury had tears in her eyes. Why so much emotion over a student from twenty years ago? Granted, the discovery of the body could have brought back memories, but Asbury didn't seem like the kind of teacher who would establish strong ties with her students. He had a vague feeling that she was hiding something.

Chapter 10

It was midnight and Asbury was roaming her home, dead drunk. She staggered past the phone and then stopped and stumbled back. She dialed a number that she knew by heart.

"Cunningham was in my office asking questions. I'm a wreck. I can't go on much longer hiding the truth. It's on my mind all day. I dream about it at night."

"What are you saying, Jillian. That you're going to confess your involvement and implicate me? You can't do that."

"I can't carry this around anymore," said the Dean.

"We must talk, Jillian. Tomorrow. I'll come over early in the morning. Take your pills. Go to sleep. Things will be better. They always are after we talk."

Jillian made it to her bedroom. Dead drunk, she dry swallowed a couple of pills and tumbled into bed.

CHAPTER 11

Cotton was getting ready to leave for work. A slight rain was staining the windows and a dense fog was shifting in when he took a phone call.

"Cotton, Jefferson Drew. Dean Asbury's dead."

Cotton froze. "I just talked to her the day before yesterday. How did it happen?"

"The police aren't exactly sure. The medical examiner is on the scene. The cleaning lady found the body in the bedroom. The little information that I have is due to a courtesy call from the Buffalo police."

"Can you call Meyerson and have him use his influence to get us into the crime scene?"

"I'll try. I'll get right back to you," said Drew.

Cotton sat down to think. It wasn't a coincidence that Asbury ended up dead less than forty-eight hours after he interviewed her about Chaz Barker's death. Even though she tried not to show it, she worked hard to suppress some inner emotion about the student. Was she directly responsible for Barker's death? Why was he murdered? If this wasn't a suicide, there was another person involved. He needed to know more about what happened twenty years ago.

Meyerson used his position as President to let Drew and Cotton into the crime scene later that day. The Buffalo Police were not happy about them being there, but the officer guarding the scene knew Cotton and it turned out to be old home week.

"Jesus, Cotton, it's been a long time," said Eddie Acoracci. They shook hands. Acoracci was a rookie during Cotton's last years as a homicide detective.

"Eddie, you don't mind if we look around a bit?" Cotton asked.

"No, go right ahead guys. I was just going to chow down on a sub. I'll be outside on the stoop. Let me know if you need anything."

The house was on a side street off Main in Amherst. Rumor had it that the State was going to build a new campus in Amherst. Plans were being drawn up in Albany to allow the University of Buffalo to become a flagship campus in the state system.

The house was a turn of the century Tudor with a curving driveway. Although the house was large, it was split up into many smaller rooms with high ceilings. Polished woodwork accented the entryway with built in bookcases on the side of the arches leading to the living room. Bay windows in the main room were lined with plants and heavily weighted chandeliers hung down in the dining and sitting rooms.

The kitchen contrasted with the other rooms and featured lime green colors and print wallpaper. Modern appliances lined the counter tops. A small eating area with French doors led to a stone patio.

"Let's split up," said Drew. "I'll take the upstairs."

Cotton nodded while he opened the refrigerator. It was apparent that the dean was not a cook. A carton of orange juice, some luncheon meat, a bottle of white wine and assorted salad fixings were all that it held.

It seemed that the Dean was either fastidious in her habits or she had a very good housekeeper. There was no clutter, no plants that were suffering and no dishes in the sink. There was an ample supply of both wine and liquor in racks to the side of the counter. There was an island in the middle of the kitchen that held both a knife block and cutting boards.

The living room held little of interest besides a leather couch, a set of rocking chairs and a fireplace that seemed to have never been lit. A coffee table was littered with magazines like The SMITHSONIAN and TRAVEL TODAY. The dining room was a separate room off the kitchen and featured a heavy table with matching chairs. On one side was a hutch that held dishes that could have been from a high-end store like Adam, Meldrum and Anderson's.

There was a small study off the living room that held an antique rolltop desk that had been opened by the police and thoroughly tossed. There were bookshelves on both sides of the desk that dealt with political thought and government. There was a telephone on a small table off to the side with a notebook next to it. He picked up the notebook and rifled through it. There were pages of names and numbers that were totally unfamiliar to Cotton. Some of them were faculty members; many were from the political science department. He copied down those names, including a phone number listed as a cottage on Crystal Beach in Canada. There was also a number that was very familiar to Cotton—The Buffalo Police Department.

Cotton finished jotting down information and joined Jefferson Drew in the upstairs bedroom where the body was found.

There was a chalk outline where the body was discovered. The bed was unmade, and clothes were strewn over the floor.

"From what I heard from my sources at the Buffalo Police Department, bottles of liquor and pills were found by the bedside. They're waiting for the toxicology report, but they're thinking suicide. From what you told me about her emotional state at your meeting and the stress she's been under, that seems reasonable," said Drew.

"I agree with what you say, but where was the stress coming from? Was it job related, or did it have something to do with Barker's death? I believe she was holding back on me."

Cotton moved over to the bathroom where a foul smell swept over him. He stepped back.

"The medical examiner said she threw up more than once during the evening," said Drew.

Cotton thought for a moment. "How many times do victims of suicide throw up?" he asked.

"I have no idea," said Drew. "Why do you ask?"

"Nothing. Just thinking aloud," said Cotton.

"According to the police, there was no suicide note and no sign of a struggle," said Drew.

"I feel like there's something wrong here, but I can't put my finger on it," said Cotton.

They continued the search without much success.

"I found some phone numbers from an address book-let that I would like to follow up on. There's a woman with the last name of Asbury that might be a sister. There's a cottage at Crystal Beach and one for the police department."

Cotton used a phone booth outside a local convenient store to make a call. It was hot and humid, and the steam clouded the plexiglass. He was calling a contact at the police department to find out if they had notified the next of kin. They had and the number matched the one from the address booklet. Her sister, Janice Asbury lived in Cleveland. Not wanting to be inappropriate, Cotton contacted Meyerson's office and got permission to contact the sister as a representative of the college.

The phone was picked up on the third ring. Cotton identified himself and offered the requisite condolences.

Janice Asbury sounded weary. "I've already talked to the police and I'm making plans to come to Buffalo. It won't be for a few days. I own a flower business and I need to get things covered. To tell you the truth, I wasn't very close to my sister. She was five years older than me, and she travelled with a totally different crowd."

"What kind of crowd was that?" asked Cotton.

"Oh, I guess you could say they were pretentious. They had to have the best clothes, go to highbrow parties. We were not wealthy. My father tended bar and my mother worked at the local American Legion post. Jill was always moaning about what she didn't have. The only reason she was able to keep up with that crowd was because of her smarts and good looks. As soon as she graduated from high school, she was off to the University of Pennsylvania. She worked hard; I'll give her that. Never came back during summer breaks. She waitressed, worked in department stores, even did a bit of modeling. She got into a fast-track graduate program and never looked back. She taught at a private school in Dayton for a few years and then got the position at the University in Buffalo."

"When was the last time you spoke to her?" asked Cotton.

"When our parents died in an automobile crash, she came back for the funeral. That was last year in September. She only stayed for a few days. There was no will so most of the time we spent dealing with the sale of the house and property. She wanted nothing to do with their possessions. She left me with all the responsibility associated with their sudden death. I was grieving and all she was concerned with was the value of the inheritance. She was heartless."

The more she talked, Cotton thought, the more she painted a picture of a highly driven woman who was narcistic and self-centered.

"Did she ever talk about her job or anything to do with her students?" asked Cotton.

Janice Asbury paused. "Why are you asking me questions about her college life? The police led me to believe she had committed suicide. Is there anything going on here that I'm not aware of?"

"The college is working closely with the police to determine the cause of death," said Cotton. "Our concern is to find out what could have led to the cause of her death. We know that she was particularly upset about the body of a former student that was unearthed on the campus grounds. All our questions are attempts to shed some light on this."

"Well, let me know what you find. In the meantime, I'll be coming to Buffalo to arrange for the funeral and find out about a possible will. I'm not trying to be sentimental about this. She really was a bitch."

<h1 style="text-align:center">CHAPTER 12</h1>

Jen Valley hooked Cotton into attending a Buffalo Philharmonic concert. It was held at Kleinhan's Music Hall, one of the better concert halls in the East. It was mid-October and Lucas Foss was the conductor. It was Mahler's Symphony #4 in G major, and Roberta Peters was the principal soprano. Cotton had hoped for something along the lines of a pop concert or perhaps music from a well-known Broadway musical, but perhaps, he thought, his attendance could be a bargaining chip for a future Buffalo Bisons baseball game.

During the intermission, she wanted to know about any progress he had made in Chaz Barker's disappearance.

"We surveyed the scene of the Dean's death and I'm still not convinced that it was a suicide. The medical examiner confirmed that it was an overdose, but there was no note. It could have been an accidental death. I found an address booklet with some phone numbers that I want to check on. I talked to her sister who admitted the Dean wasn't a very loving person. I found a phone number of a cottage in Canada. I don't know if the cottage was hers. There's a lot of leg work to do and I've got college classes to attend to. Meyerson says he could cut down my load, but I'd hate to do that. I took this teaching job to get away from all this."

Jen smiled and patted his hand. "You didn't get much

of a breather after last year's tragedy. Then you helped me recuperate."

"I never regretted my time at the hospital with you," he said with a smile. "I'll manage. There's a part of all this that gets my adrenaline flowing. After all, it beats lecturing about the Nullification Crisis."

"Hey, don't knock the Nullification Crisis. After all, it's not every day that a President threatens to hang his vice-president to a tree."

That got Cotton laughing. His lectures were listless since Chaz Barker's body was discovered. He missed the satisfaction of a class well taught, and conversations that could make a difference in a student's life.

The second half of the concert began, and Cotton was glad that it was one of Mahler's shortest works.

Chapter 13

The next day, Cotton was in his office early. His window was open due to the unseasonably warm weather. It was close to the turn of the hour and noises of students making the passage between classes filled the air. He was making a phone call to Chaz Barker's brother. The younger Barker lived in his parents' home in Gambier, Ohio, the home of Kenyon College. He answered in a gravelly voice.

Ned was glad to share information. "When Chaz disappeared, we all travelled to Buffalo and stayed in a motel for almost two weeks waiting for any information from the police. It wasn't like Chaz to just take off without letting somebody know. He called home every Sunday night, mostly to discuss his thesis with Dad. I lived at home at the time. I had recently graduated from Kenyon with a business degree. We were disappointed in the police progress and came home feeling that we should have learned more. My parents were never the same after that. My father even travelled back to Buffalo every few months to meet with the police. He would walk around the college, drive past his apartment, even ate at some of the restaurants that Chaz had frequented. It aged him. He lived another ten years after that but retired early and just vegetated. My mother tried to lift him up, but her health was failing at the time. They died within months of each other, a broken couple."

"Mr. Barker, did Chaz ever mention anything to you about anyone who held a grudge against him, anyone at the college that he didn't get along with?"

"The police went over that with me and I told them that I had no idea of any animosity between Chaz and any other person, community or campus."

"Did Chaz ever talk to you about his thesis advisor?" asked Cotton.

"He mentioned that he worked with a woman in the political science department. I remembered his saying that she wanted to work with him on a future publication, but that he wasn't interested. He was working with Dad on developing his thesis into a book."

Cotton picked right up on this idea. "Do you know how the woman felt about this? Was there any friction between the two?"

"That was the last time we spoke. Do you think there is any connection between this woman and Chaz's death?" asked Ned.

"I'm not sure, but after Chaz's body was discovered, the woman was found dead from an overdose," said Cotton

"There has to be something to that!" said Ned. "That can't be just a coincidence."

"I'm beginning to think so," said Cotton. "Do you know where I can get a copy of your brother's thesis?"

"That's another strange issue. When the police searched his apartment, there was evidence of his work, but no thesis," said Ned.

"You said your father worked with him on the thesis?" asked Cotton

"Yes, quite closely," said Ned.

"Is there any chance there might be something left behind in your father's papers that would explain what Chaz was working on?" asked Cotton.

There was silence on the phone. "I never thought about looking through Dad's papers," said Ned. "He was a prolific writer. All his papers are in the basement of our family house. There must be six file cabinets."

"Would you have a problem with me coming down and looking through his papers?" asked Cotton.

"No, of course not, but if it would help, I could do that in my spare time. Anything I could do to shed some light on my brother's murder would give me much needed closure. His murder destroyed our family. I'll start on it tomorrow."

The phone conversation with Ned Barker gave Cotton some threads to pull on and he was going to start pulling hard. It would begin with interviewing some faculty members who were there twenty years ago.

Chapter 14

Thornton Delaware was a professor in the Political Science department. Cotton had done his homework and figured that Delaware was a senior Political Science major the year Barker had disappeared. He might have known Chaz Barker and certainly knew of the publicity surrounding his disappearance. He made an appointment and was waiting outside his office when the professor arrived toting a satchel. He was dressed professorially in khaki pants, corduroy jacket with patches on the elbows, a striped dress shirt with a paisley tie. A pipe was clenched in his hand. He was slim, with a salon haircut and an air of upper class. He had a noticeable limp.

"Cunningham, let me use my key and let you in."

A click of the lock and he ushered Cotton into an office that was more like a living room in a palatial mansion. There was a huge oak desk that dominated the room in front of a double set of windows. On the desk were paper weights, a rack of pipes and In and Out wooden boxes. On the walls were framed campaign posters, pictures of Delaware on safari in Africa and mountain climbing in some remote region.

He waved Cotton into a chair in front of his desk, sat down and made a tent with his fingers.

"How can I help you?" he asked

Cotton had no professional relationship with Delaware. He seldom saw him on campus and never served on any committees with him.

"Dr. Delaware, I represent Martin Meyerson in the affair of the body that was uncovered on campus. It was determined that the student, Chaz Barker, had been a doctoral student in 1948. I realize you were an undergrad back then, and I'm wondering whether you remember Barker or the incident."

"I do remember the incident. I was even questioned about the matter by the police. It was true that I was an undergraduate at the time, but undergraduates rarely mix with doctoral students. They run with a different crowd and if they are completing coursework, it's at a different time of day. I did not know the unfortunate lad."

"We have reason to believe that there might be a connection between the discovery of the body and the death of Dean Asbury," said Cotton.

Delaware was fumbling with his pipe, loading it with tobacco.

"A tragic affair, Jillian's death.I took classes from her during that time. And later taught with her in the Political Science department. She was an excellent instructor and a fine dean, but how would that be related to Barker's death?"

"She was Barker's faculty advisor. When I interviewed her about the discovery of the body, she was quite upset. Her death occurred shortly after," said Cotton.

Delaware sat back in his chair. "The talk around the department is that she committed suicide," Delaware said. "Is there any reason to think otherwise?"

"The police have been thinking along those lines, but nothing has been ruled out," said Cotton. "Was she under any pressure that you know of? Had she been despondent or conflicted in any way?"

"Not that I know of," Delaware said.

"Are there any other faculty members who might shed any light on this matter?" asked Cotton.

Delaware paused for a moment. "Elsbeth Scott was a student with me at the time and she is a colleague of mine in the Political Science department."

"Thank you for your time, Dr. Delaware. If you can think of anything else that might be helpful, you can contact me on my faculty office phone," said Cotton.

Delaware escorted Cotton to his door, shut it after him and waited a moment before picking up his phone and dialing.

"Hello, Elsbeth, he just left my office, and he should be contacting you soon. He wants to know about Barker. He's trying to make a connection between Barker and Jillian. No, no they haven't made any connection between you and Jillian or Barker. It would help if we got our stories straight. I'll come over to your house tonight. Is Jackson still away on business? Good, I'll see you around nine."

Delaware lit one of his pipes, took a draw and thought. The body was found buried in a place far away from the main campus. Now, with a person like Cunningham perusing leads, the situation was touchy. But, if everyone kept calm, they should be all right.

Chapter 15

Cotton's nephew Teddy loved Griffith's Sculpture Park. It was 425 acres of an outdoor art museum. For a Down Syndrome child like Teddy, it could have been an overdose of color, but for some reason, he loved it. There was room to run and that's what he enjoyed. The park had been built in 1966 and was the first sculpture park in the United States. It was in East Otto, near Ellicottville, a tourist town and ski resort. It was especially stunning in autumn, when the brilliant colors stood in stark contrast to the tall metal sculptures. Teddy would stop and stare and run. When he finally got home to Cotton's sister, Brittany, Teddy would be worn out and ready for bed.

Brittany had called Cotton the night before and pleaded with him to give her a childcare break. It was Saturday and Cotton made time. When Teddy was born, most of the family had considered him a burden. Cotton considered him a blessing. Generally good natured, with an infectious smile, he was a boy in constant motion.

Cotton's father, who was incapacitated in a Buffalo nursing home, thought Teddy should be put into a group home with the other "retards." Cotton had a contentious relationship with his father who thought Cotton should have never given up his job with the police department. He was disdainful of academics who he thought were effeminate and unmanly. Brittany was a loving mother who was weary from taking care of three children. Her husband Fred, a liquor salesman, liked his time with the guys, be it a softball game or a carouse in a south town's bar. He was a monetary provider but an absentee father.

People called Teddy simple, but if simple meant uncomplicated, without ulterior motives, free of pettiness and maliciousness, then Cotton could handle simple. There had been family discussions about a home for special children. He would fight to keep Teddy from being institutionalized because he knew what that meant. Cotton had handled many cases where children like Teddy were neglected and even abused. Teddy needed his family.

As Teddy ran, so did Cotton's thoughts. If Asbury didn't commit suicide, was she murdered? To keep her quiet. Quiet about what? Chaz Barker's death would be a logical assumption. And why was Barker murdered? Cotton thought it all centered around Dean Asbury. She was the center. Who were the characters swirling around her? Cotton had not talked to enough people. The cottage in Canada had to be investigated.

Every time that Cotton went out with Teddy, it always ended up with ice cream. Today it was a small stand in Ellicottville. Teddy opted for a rainbow cone. As usual, half ended up on the table, but it was glorious fun.

When he dropped off Teddy that afternoon, he had a short talk with his sister.

"Fred thinks we should investigate a home for Teddy, something that meets his needs. I think he belongs here and I'm going to fight him on this."

"I'm totally with you on this, Brit. What he needs is love, safety and understanding. He gets those from you. He's a happy child here."

"Fred says that an institutionalized setting will get him the training that he needs for later in life," said Brittany.

"Brit, he's only six years old. There will be plenty of time to think about that when he's a teenager," said Cotton.

"Talk to Fred, Cotton. He's says that we'll be able to do more things together, the two of us if we didn't have the burden. He's hardly ever around. I wonder if he stays away because of Teddy. Cotton, I want my husband back."

"I'll talk to him, Brit, don't worry," said Cotton.

He thought to himself, *don't do it, Brit. Don't do it.*

Chapter 16

Cotton was called into Marty Meyerson's office the next day for a briefing. "What do you have for me on Barker?" he asked.

"Nothing solid, but I think Barker's death and the deans are connected somehow. I've talked to several people, and I get the feeling that there's something missing – something that's not adding up."

"You mean a gut feeling?" asked Meyerson.

"I know what you're getting at. My gut isn't going to solve your problems."

Meyerson sighed. "I know you're doing the best you can, but I have to deal with disgruntled parents and alumni. They want answers. They want a simple solution so we can get back to normal."

'I've got more leads to follow up and people I need to run down. I'm not giving up on this," said Cotton.

"Remember Cotton, you're not police anymore."

Chapter 17

Cotton must have been feeling the pressure because the next day found him crossing the Peace bridge into Canada on his way to Crystal Beach.

Crystal Beach, Ontario was the home of one of the largest amusement parks in the area. It was also a community where many U.S. citizens owned property. Cotton's map reading skills were rusty and he stopped off at more than one general store for directions before pulling into the driveway. He made calls to both Jillian's sister and the Buffalo police and had gotten a key from Jillian's lawyer. He was hoping that there was something here to provide some answers.

When Cotton pulled into the driveway, it was not a cottage he was facing but a huge Victorian edifice. The outside was weathered but still retained the grandeur of previous years. It was a three-story affair with bay windows surrounding the first floor and a wraparound porch that commanded views in many directions. On this autumn day, Lake Erie loomed across the street in blueish grey waves. The lawn was overgrown, as if the maintenance service had been discontinued. White rocking chairs and a porch swing swayed in the cool breeze. Leaves scattered on the porch and collected between the screen door and the interior entrance. There was an air of abandonment and disuse. It was full of the past but no presence.

Cotton climbed the porch as a gust of wind opened and slammed shut the screen door. It took him a good five minutes to get the key to work, alternately pressing and pulling the key in the lock. It finally opened onto a lengthy hallway which led to the back of the house. Off to the side was a sitting room, possibly for entertaining and on the left a more modern living room featuring a fireplace with bookshelves on either side. The sofas and chairs were covered with white sheets and the walls with both watercolors and oils depicting seascapes and turn of the century tourists' scenes on the beach. There was a supply of kindling and larger logs even though the fireplace was fitted for gas.

There was a coffee table in front of the couch with assorted magazines—COUNTRY LIFE, The NEW YORKER and the NEW YORK TIMES MAGAZINE. Cotton checked the dates. They were from early summer.

The kitchen was large and seemed to be missing most modern accoutrements. There was a coffee maker, some cookbooks on a shelf and a narrow tray filled with the detritus of unopened mail. Local notices about garage sales, community gatherings and 4th of July fireworks lay on the counter. There was a bulletin board with the phone numbers of takeout restaurants. What attracted Cotton's attention the most was a faded photograph that featured an outdoor scene, perhaps a barbecue. In it were six people. A much younger Jillian Asbury, a dashing Thornton Delaware, a woman and man who looked vaguely familiar, a black man in shorts and a tall woman in capris that Cotton recognized as Dolores Davis.

They were posed in what seemed to be a very cordial way. Cotton looked hard at the two people who looked familiar. They were both UB people, but he couldn't place them.

He continued through the house, quickly into the dining room and a stairway near the front door. The creaky stairs led to a landing that offered a generous view of the lake. He proceeded upstairs to the second floor which featured five bedrooms – two on one side and three on the other with a communal bathroom on one side. He checked out four of them which were obvious guest rooms and of little interest to him, and a master bedroom with its own bathroom which he assumed was used by Jillian Asbury. The bathroom featured a clawfoot bathtub with a wraparound shower curtain. The counter had a small sample of cosmetics in a basket with shampoo and conditioner. There was a medicine cabinet that held a bottle of aspirin, nail clippers, brush, and a generic bottle of sleep aids.

The pictures in the bedroom were like the ones in the living room. It struck Cotton that there was nothing on the walls of the house to signify family or friends or any other emotional attachments. Nothing in the rest of the upstairs was useful to him. He continued to a small series of steps that led to a door. He ascended the steps and turned the door handle. This obviously was an attic, with a lack of conventional floorboards, only joists with asbestos between them. There were boxes placed across the joists. Cotton sighed. A trip through a musty attic to go through age old boxes had not been on his agenda.

Still, it needed to be done and perhaps a quick inspection of the first few boxes would prove useful. He straddled the two by sixes and duck walked over to the first of the boxes. There was a small window at the end of the attic that provided some light. He opened the first box and found old kitchen ware, lights, and extension cords. He continued to the next box and found out it was a repository for old NATIONAL GEOGRAPHIC magazines. *Must weigh a ton* thought Cotton. He made his way through two more boxes with no luck until he found something of interest—a collection of academic articles.

Being a teacher, Cotton was familiar with such writings. Many of them were in their early forms with spelling mistakes and crossed out words. Many with Jillian Asbury's name on them. He wanted to inspect them, but the dim light and musty interior forced him to drag the box precariously over the timbers and down the few steps to the solid floor. He continued down the steps to the first floor and out the door to his car.

Before he left, he wanted to look at the books to either side of the fireplace. Surprisingly, they were less academic than he thought and even featured several READER'S DIGEST condensed books. Wedged into a corner of the bookshelf was something that caught his attention. It was a small book with Jillian Asbury's name on it. Its title was of a political nature, something combining politics and economics. Cotton tucked it under his arm, locked the house, confident that he had done his best to ferret out any useful evidence.

That night, over a Molson's, he would read some of the material to become familiar with Asbury's writing style. Although most doctoral students and their advisor's relationships were professional, he had a suspicion that Asbury and Barker's had led to murder.

Chapter 18

He was in his office the next day, preparing for his ten o'clock class. Piles of papers were accumulating throughout the room. The door was open and the noise of students and faculty going about their daily rounds made it hard to concentrate. The was a lull in the traffic when Cassandra Day walked in. She was in style with a red striped turban on her head and huge, hooped earrings. She had madras bell bottoms with a black turtleneck sweater.

"Came by to do some work in my office and thought I would stop to see how things were going with this case you've been working on," she said.

"Slow going for sure," said Cotton, motioning for her to sit. "I still need to talk with some people around campus who were teaching back then."

"There aren't that many of us left, "she said with a chuckle.

"By the way," said Cotton, "You would be a good person to show this to." He reached for his briefcase and pulled out the faded picture from Asbury's summer home. He handed it to her. "I recognize the Dean and Dolores Davis but the black man, young woman and short guy, they look familiar, but I can't place them."

She took the picture and studied it for a moment. "The young woman is Elsbeth Scott from the Political Science department," she said.

"Of course, now I recognize her. Her hair is much longer now," said Cotton.

"The black man is a tough one. You would have never found out who he is. His name is Acton Powers, and he was a history professor back in the late forties. He taught for a couple of years but never received tenure. He was quite a revolutionary. He was into Black Power before Black Power was a thing. I think his politics was too much for the college.

"What ever happened to him?" asked Cotton.

"He's still around. I think he runs a bookstore on the east side. Goes by a Muslim name now," said Day.

"More people to interview. I'm trying to figure out how they all fit together," said Cotton.

"As I recall that group did hang out together. Except for Dolores, they were about the same age," said Day.

"Thanks," said Cotton. "I've got to take off for my 10:00 class. Glad you stopped by. You've given me more threads to pull."

"No problem," said Cassandra." Let me know if I can help. Keep me in the loop."

Later that day, he was lounging on his back deck, cradling a bottle of Molson Golden, when he heard the phone ring. It was Chaz Barker's brother.

"Good news. I've been looking through my father's papers and I found a copy of part of my brother's thesis. He worked on it with my father and dad gave him plenty of advice. They were constantly mailing back and forth with revisions. I think Dad hoped he could eventually turn it into a book. I could send it to you if you'd like. I worked on it with my father."

"Definitely," said Cotton. "If you find anything else even remotely connected to the thesis, send that also."

More reading material, thought Cotton. The more he thought about it, it seemed like there was murder within these ivy halls.

Chapter 19

It was a Saturday in October, and Cotton was cashing in his Gustav Mahler chips. He and Jen were attending a UB football game versus Delaware. UB coach Doc Ulrich was pacing the sidelines on the warm, slightly overcast day. The stands were full of UB students drinking from paper bags. The whiff of marijuana was in the air and a pleasant time was had by all.

"There's something special about a Saturday afternoon football game in October with the fall foliage and the cheers of the crowd," said Jen.

"Nature's first green is gold, her hardest hue to hold, her early leaf's a flower, but only so an hour, then leaf subsides to leaf, so Eden sank to grief, so dawn goes down today, nothing gold can stay."

"Cunningham, you old romantic, that's Robert Frost," said Jen.

"Yes, it is and many thanks to Mr. Jeffries my high school teacher. He was big on memorizing poems. It took me a while to realize that the ability to recite something from memory is a gift you can always hold on to."

Just then a roar came up from the crowd as Rutkowski plowed into the endzone for UB's first score.

"Not to break the spell of collegiate spirit, how's the investigation going?" asked Jen, sipping on a diet soda.

Cotton was munching on a bag of peanuts and drinking a Royal Crown soda. "I feel like I'm being pulled in twenty different directions. My classes, Chaz Barker and now Brittany's husband is putting pressure on her to institutionalize Teddy."

"Oh, Cotton, I know how you feel about the boy. There's got to be a way to convince them that putting him in a home is not the answer," said Jen.

"The problem is that Fred's staying out to all hours and avoiding his family. He says that if Teddy goes, then their marriage would be much more salvageable. Brittany must choose between her husband and her son. It's a lousy choice and it's not fair to Teddy."

"What can we do?" asked Jen.

"I'm going to talk to Fred. I want him to know what this will mean to Teddy. Some of these places do not attract the most caring human beings," said Cotton.

Changing the subject, Jen asked about his classes.

"I'm down to three because Meyerson wants to give me more time to be his representative to the student body, which means more time to work on Chaz Barker's disappearance. The three classes are interesting. The ten o'clock class is docile, without much discussion going on. The 2:30 class is off the wall funny and has me in stiches half the time. And the evening class is feisty and wants to argue over every issue. A lot of the students in that class walk the picket lines during the day. They want to enlist me, but so far, I've been able to stay out of the fray."

"I'm afraid I haven't been able to resist. I've been marching with my students over Project Themis. I sincerely believe that the Department of Defense project should not be on campus."

"I understand your objections. I just believe that my

job is to initiate civil discourse. There are those who believe our country is racist. I believe race is a critical factor in the study of history. I welcome discussion of these issues in my class. Capitalism has made our country great, but at the same time, it has produced many depressions where people suffered. There is also the topic of income inequality. The movement west led to many wonderful achievements, but displaced thousands of Indians. Our country is replete with stories of injustice, but also filled with heroism," said Cotton.

Another cheer went up as Dennis Mason completed a touchdown pass which put UB up by two scores.

"How's the investigation?" she asked.

"Slow going. A lot of interviews. Elsbeth Scott from Political Science was a student back then and later a friend of Dean Asbury. I found a picture of her at the Crystal Beach house that may prove useful. There's a black man in the picture who taught history in the late forties and was denied tenure. He's a bookstore owner on the east side.

UB beat Delaware by the score of 29-17. As they walked out of the stadium arm in arm, the college clock rang the hour.

"How about dinner at Cambria's and then a night cap at my apartment? Who knows how far that will go?" said Cotton.

"Yes, who knows," said Jen with a twinkle in her eye.

Chapter 20

Cotton's appointment with Elsbeth Scott was the following Monday after his last class. Political Science was just down the hall from the history department, so he dropped a few things in his office, watered the geranium that Jen had given him last Christmas, and proceeded to Scott's office. He knew the secretary and stopped off to say hello. She had a daughter who was disabled, and she was familiar with Cotton's nephew Teddy. When he told her who he was there to see, she told him, "Second door on the left." She rolled her eyes and turned up her nose. Cotton understood the gesture.

Scott's door was closed. He knocked and waited for a response. After a second a low voice muttered, "Come in."

Cotton opened the door and walked into a room that reeked of pretense. The furniture was not campus issued. The couch on one side of the room was black leather with a white fuzzy throw over it. Two chrome chairs faced an oak desk that almost spanned the width of the room. Antique feather pens protruded from ink wells on either corner of the desk. A dictionary sat on a stand to one side and on the wall opposite, there were bookshelves that held hard covers and paperbacks. There was a white sheepskin rug that looked like it shouldn't be stepped on. Scott sat behind the desk.

She was dressed in a pink mohair sweater. She had

multiple rings on both hands and nails that were long and dark. Strangely enough, Cotton thought, she looked like she hadn't aged at all from the picture in Asbury's summer house. Her hair was dark, almost black and her skin a flawless porcelain. Eyelashes were long and lips a dark red. She was an attractive woman, the only thing detracting from her beauty was a cruel twist of her mouth.

"Dr. Cunningham, I don't think we've been formally introduced," she said.

"We've met at various college functions but never spoke," he said. "Thank you for taking time out of your schedule to meet with me."

"I'm sure this has something to do with the untimely death of our beloved dean."

"Yes, it does," said Cotton. "Her death and the unfortunate death of a student from twenty years ago whose body was recently discovered. The president asked me to investigate the matter."

"Ah, yes," said Scott." You are, as I remember, the President's hired gun?"

Cotton smiled. The sarcasm was obvious. "My position is not quite as dramatic as that, Dr. Scott. I am a special assistant to the President, tasked with dealing with problems concerning the student body. Most of my interventions are quite innocuous."

"The murders on campus last year can hardly be called innocuous," said Scott. "It was the talk of the campus community."

"A very unfortunate series of events," said Cotton. "Believe me when I say that I am much more comfortable in front of a classroom of students than dealing with police matters."

"And yet, you did that for many years, I've been told. Don't you miss the thrill of the chase?"

The woman was on the offensive. Cotton knew that he had to switch the conversation.

"How well did you know the Dean during your undergraduate years?" he asked.

For some reason, the question took her aback. She recovered quickly. "I took classes from the dean when she was a young professor. She was an excellent teacher who pushed her students to excel."

"Were you aware of the disappearance of Chaz Barker when he was a student?" Cotton asked.

"It was quite the news on campus at the time. The police questioned many students and professors. I was an undergraduate, so I had no contact with him."

"Did you remember if the disappearance had any effect on the Dean?" he asked.

"In what way?" she asked defensively. "We were all saddened by the matter."

"Did she seem shaken or upset at the time?" Cotton asked.

"The only time I associated with her was in class and I don't think the matter ever came up," she answered.

"Did you notice any change in her demeanor in the days preceding her death?"

"My association with her was mainly at faculty meetings at the beginning of the semester. We have both been busy since."

Cotton produced the photo that he had taken from the summer home of Asbury and laid it in front of her. At first, she seemed unmoved and then she straightened up stiffly.

"Where did you get this picture," she demanded.

"You know the people in this picture?" he asked.

At first, she didn't reply. Then she grudgingly nodded. "Yes, some of them. This picture must have been taken years ago. They're all colleagues of mine from the college. Except the Negro. I don't recall who he was."

"Let me refresh your memory. His name was Acton Powers. He was a professor at the college until he lost a tenure battle."

"I don't have a recollection of that," she said nervously.

"He changed his name. Maybe he can provide me with some information," said Cotton.

Scott's expression was cold.

"Thank you very much, Dr. Scott. At this point, we are trying to ascertain whether Dean Asbury's death was a suicide."

"I mourn her death, Dr. Cunningham, but I'm afraid I can't help you in that regard."

Cotton left her office no further ahead in the investigation than he was before. It seemed like all the characters in this story were closing ranks.

Chapter 21

Cotton received a box in the mail the next day from Chaz's brother. "*Oh, man, he thought, I've got a lot of reading to do.*" He opened the box and found a partial copy of Chaz's thesis entitled *The Effects of Insider Trading Information On the Public Conscience.* It totaled 143 pages. Sifting quickly through the box, he found letters written back and forth between father and son. To say that the father was interested in his son's work was an understatement. The letters were all one way, from son to father

At first, the son replied to his father in a deferential way befitting a mentor student relationship. As time went on, Chaz's tone became more defensive and even combative, objecting to some of the advice the father was doling out. At one point, he even stated, "I'm the one writing this paper. I'm not an extension of you. My thoughts don't need to be dissected."

Good for you, Cotton thought. *Don't take any crap from the old man.* Cotton had a lot to read, not just Chaz's work, but Jillian Asbury's also. He had a thought swimming in the back of his mind, but he couldn't pull it out. This was night work—after he taught his classes, graded papers, and talked to other people involved in the case. And he had to carve out time for a promising relationship with Jen. There wasn't enough time in the day.

Chapter 22

Brittany phoned him on the phone the next day. "Cotton, Fred and I are going to be looking at some group homes for Teddy this week. He did the leg work, researched, and found a couple nice places. The cost would be covered by the state. We're talking again and it feels good."

Cotton could barely catch his breath. When he did, he exploded. "I can't believe you're thinking of kicking him out of your home! He's your child, just as much as your daughters are."

As soon as he said that he regretted it.

His sister was now in tears. "I can't believe you said that. You don't know what it's like to raise a child like Teddy. You have him once every few weeks and have a grand time. You don't have him when he shits in his pants or refuses to eat anything but pizza. You never see the hard side, the side that I must do alone because my husband can't be bothered. Now I have a chance to have a marriage again and you have a problem with that. Well fuck off!"

And she hung up.

Well, I screwed that up, thought Cotton. *She came to me for some support, and I let off steam. I'll let it go for a few days and then call her back and apologize.* He needed to talk to Fred, try to reason with him. He didn't need this scene. He didn't have the time. But Teddy...

THAT night Cotton worked on the material that Chaz's brother sent. The windows were open, and the sounds of city streets drifted in. Car horns, wheels peeling and the barely audible sound of traffic lights changing were second nature noises to Cotton.

He didn't have a separate room as a study, but he did have a massive, antique dining table. He liked spreading things out on the table—a good workstation. First, he began reading the dissertation. It was a combination of politics and economics, two fields that Cotton was unfamiliar with. He had a basic knowledge of both fields, but this was complex. He slugged through it with coffee breaks in between. He kept music on in the background – low volume rock. He stopped after a hundred pages. He thought he might read some of the letters Chaz wrote to his father.

It was easier reading, but still dealt with some dense material. Interspersed with the thesis comments, there was some ordinary banter—the weather, where he had been eating, the occasional date, nothing serious. It seemed like the only thing Chaz was serious about was his thesis and how he could get out of what he called, "this hole of a city."

Chaz did mention his relationship with his faculty advisor—a person he referred to as a "lazy academic." According to Chaz, her advice was generic and not very helpful. Her knowledge of economics was minimal, and she wasn't very available. She cancelled out on appointments more than once and one time she didn't show up. Chaz was not impressed with Jillian Asbury.

Suddenly, things changed in their relationship. A month before Chaz disappeared, Asbury started to show more interest in Chaz's work and their meetings became more frequent and detailed. She asked questions about his sources and the ideas he was discussing with his father.

In the last letter that he ever sent to his father, shortly after the new year, he related how he was becoming suspicious of her newfound interest.

Cotton put down the letters and checked his watch. 1:15 in the morning. He could push on, but he would be a wreck the next day. He left his workstation wondering about Chaz's relationship with Jillian Asbury.

Chapter 23

He was walking into his office the next day when he was approached by Jack Larson, the history department chairman. Jack was in his early fifties, overweight and balding. He was firmly entrenched in the bureaucracy of college politics and in Cotton's opinion, not at all interested in students or history.

"Cotton, can a have a word with you?" he asked.

"Sure, Jack, what's up?"

"I know Marty has you working hard on Asbury's death. That's very time consuming and I'm concerned that it might be taking its toll on your classroom duties."

Cotton knew where this was heading. Larson's wife was an adjunct in the department, and he would like nothing better than to hand over some of Cotton's courses to his wife.

"I'm fine, Jack. My classes aren't suffering. And I don't believe my students have a problem with my teaching. Check out my evaluation forms. I think you'll find them very positive."

"Ok, Cotton. Just wanted to be sure. The department needs to be stable you know. "He wandered down the hallway, muttering to himself. Cotton just shook his head and unlocked his office.

Cotton liked his office neat, but he wasn't obsessive. There were piles of papers on his desk, chairs were not aligned perfectly, and he didn't have his books organized by author. Other than that, he was neat, according to an old girlfriend," for a guy."

He had just settled in when there was a knock on his door. He looked up and saw Jimmy Salukis, a senior history major and one of Cotton's favorite students. Jimmy overcame a hardscrabble childhood in the Bronx that consisted of homeless shelters, drugs, and gang wars. He made it through high school thanks to a varsity basketball coach who took him in after his sophomore year and encouraged him both in athletics and in the classroom. He entered the army after high school, engaged in combat and earned both a Bronze Star and Purple Heart for valor on the battlefield. In the classroom, he was always involved in constructive discussions. He was an advocate for the poor, organizing countless food drives and serving in food pantries.

"Hey, Jimmy, what's up?" asked Cotton.

"Do you have a minute, Dr. Cunningham? I have a problem I needed to talk to you about."

"Sure, Jimmy. Sit down."

Jimmy lowered his six-foot four-inch frame into a chair, his legs stretched out. He wore a UB sweatshirt, jeans, and Converse sneakers.

Cotton opened his hands as a signal for Jimmy to begin.

"You know all the protesting that's going on around campus the last few years with the war and all; students marching and planning protests. Most of them are peaceful, but some of them advocate violence. I'm friends with some and they ask me to join their protests. I've fought in the war, and I believe in everyone's right to oppose it, but I believe in some things they oppose. I believe in having

ROTC on campus and I don't have a problem with Project Themis. I'm being pushed by a lot of these people."

"Jimmy, you know I served in Korea, don't you?" asked Cunningham.

Jimmy looked surprised. "No, I didn't."

"For two years. Shipped back when I was wounded and used the G.I. Bill to pay for my college. Protests were just starting when I was going to school and some of the students were very wary of me being a veteran. I was smacked more than once by a snowball."

"How did you deal with it?" asked Salukis.

"I was honest about it. Told them that I fought in a war that I believed in. It was different back then. Korea wasn't Viet Nam. I'm pretty much aligned with your thinking, Jimmy. I don't believe I should join in marching because I believe as a teacher, I shouldn't be taking sides. I think my job is to be in the classroom leading discussions. I think these are issues that should be part of the classroom." Jimmy stood up and extended his hand. They shook. "Thanks a lot. I don't know if you solved my problem, but it's good to know there are others that faced the same thing."

Chapter 24

Later that night, he tackled his readings again. Things were piling up in his living room. His normal cleaning schedule was interrupted by the extra work that he had taken on. Unread newspapers, clothes and the normal detritus of a bachelor filled the room.

This time he included some of the papers that he took from the Dean's summer home. There was a bound copy of her own dissertation that dealt with the filibuster. He skimmed through that, but he was more interested in papers that occurred within the time frame of Chaz's disappearance.

It seemed that Asbury hit a dry spell and had no publications after her dissertation, except for a few articles published in the Buffalo papers. Then, in 1949, an article published in a scholarly journal entitled, "Insider Trading, the Moral Implications."

Now, Cotton had a bone to chew.

THE next morning, Cotton was in President Meyerson's office along with Jefferson Drew, head of security. He was drinking his second cup of coffee to stay awake.

"So, you believe that Asbury was involved in the theft of intellectual property from a graduate student?" Meyerson asked.

"That's what I think," replied Cotton. "The plagiarism

isn't obvious, and it might not stand up in a legal battle, but it's too much of a coincidence. There was nothing that was lifted directly from Barker's dissertation, but the ideas, the suggestions and the final conclusions were the same."

"So, this gives us a very strong suspect in the death of Chaz Barker," said Drew.

"Perhaps," said Meyerson. "But it raises another question."

"I agree," said Cotton." If she killed Barker, who killed her and why?"

"Simple," said Drew. "She kills Barker and buries the body and then when the body is discovered, she feels remorse and commits suicide."

Cotton frowned. "She killed Barker because he discovered she stole his dissertation? That's a little much, don't you think? A junkie would kill for a fix, but why would an academic, someone who worked for years to get a position at a prestigious college, decide that murder was a cure for writer's block."

They all looked at each other. "I think it goes deeper than stolen intellectual property," said Cotton. "I would like to look into this further, with your permission," said Cotton.

Meyerson sighed. "We have a plausible solution to our problem, and I think that we shouldn't make public the fact that a dean at our university was guilty of intellectual theft. I'm thinking about how that would make our university look. Nothing is gained by making that public. The police view this as a suicide. Will any kind of justice be served by a further investigation?"

Cotton was afraid of this. Meyerson was a good man, but he was furiously devoted to the college, and the college, when you get down to it, is essentially image. The right image meant alumni support. A bad image could take years to overcome.

"Cotton, I want justice to be served, but until I get definitive proof that Dean Asbury committed a crime, I will not publicly accuse her. I will, of course, turn over everything we have discovered to the police and let them proceed as they will. Return to the classroom, Cotton. It's your first love and you're damn good at it."

Cunningham and Drew left Meyerson's office in silence. As they exited the building, Drew turned to Cotton.

"Well?" asked Drew. "I know you, Cotton. You've never left the cop behind."

"There's more to this. I know there is. But I think if I keep pulling on this, part of the college will unravel. That's not what I want. I want a nice easy solution that ties everything up in a neat bow," said Cotton.

They both laughed.

Chapter 25

Harry Hathaway was holding a party at his lakefront home in Wanakah. He was ready to put his boat in storage and was inviting any intrepid souls who wished to freeze their butts off to accompany him in that task. In return, hamburgers, and hotdogs for all! It was a social sciences faculty party – bring a dish to pass and the kegs of beer would be opened. He pegged the weather forecast just right – in the high sixties. His home was a spacious ranch with a huge back lawn that ended in a break wall overlooking a stretch of private beach.

"It's gorgeous," said Jen Valley. "Maybe we should be looking for property out here."

"*Hmm, thought Cotton. She's making plans for us*". He was thinking of buying a house outside the city. They could move to Amherst, although that was a little too preppy for a city boy. Or they could go southtowns, with plenty of acceptable places to choose from – Hamburg, Eden, the Boston Hills. Cotton had a police pension plus his salary as a teacher. He wasn't affluent, but with money he had saved, they could afford a house in the suburbs.

"Cunningham where are you?" a voice cried out.

When he came back from his housing daydreams, he was staring at Ben Justice, a colleague from the history department. He had taken grad classes with Ben as they followed parallel paths to their doctorates and eventual teaching positions. Ben was Black, grew up in Cleveland

and went to Case Western for his undergrad. He came to UB for its reputation in History.

"Ben, sorry. I guess I was somewhere else," said Cotton.

Jen had gone off to speak with one of her coworkers and had left Cotton alone with his dreams.

"Must be Meyerson has you running around in circles," said Ben.

"Just a bit," said Cotton. "What have you been working on?"

"Middle States Assessment. I'm chairing the committee. It's one committee that I promise you don't want to be on, "he said.

Middle States was a governing body that handed out accreditation to hundreds of colleges and universities that conferred undergraduate and graduate degrees. It was treated very carefully by the college.

"How are Bernice and the kids?" asked Cotton.

"Just fine, Cotton and a third Justice is on its way."

"Hey, man, congratulations!" replied Cotton.

Cotton remembered when Ben was finishing up his dissertation. Two kids and a wife who worked in the admissions department almost put Ben over the edge.

"When the third one pops, I think Bernice is going to be a stay-at-home mom. The daycare would be too expensive, and it would be a grind taking them in the morning."

"It sounds complicated, Ben. Maybe you need a flow chart."

"Thankfully, Bernice is very organized," said Ben.

"Not to get off the topic, but you've worked with some Political Science people on committees, haven't you?" asked Cotton.

"Yes, I have," Ben replied.

"Ever work with Elsbeth Scott?" Cotton asked.

Ben whistled. "The cool witch? That's what they call her. Her good looks intimidate men, but not me. I'm bulletproof."

"Seriously, though, what did you think of her?"

"Smart, with an attitude. Dresses like Madison Avenue. Been at the college for years and expects the perks. Hangs out with another professor from Political Science name of Delaware. She's married but they act like a couple. Why do you ask?"

"I interviewed them both over the Barker case. They both claimed they didn't know him," said Cotton.

"Sorry, buddy. I can't help you with that. But now that I think about it, there's another guy they hang with – a fellow from the printing department. A short, stocky guy, not very sociable."

"What's his name?" Cotton.

"Bowers," said Ben. "But I think he's a hanger on, like a fan, if you know what I mean."

"I get the picture," said Cotton.

They continued talking, mostly about the graduate student days and the grind that goes with it. Then the burgers were coming off the grill and the chow line was forming. People congregated in line and Cotton and Jen found themselves next to Edison Texidor from Anthropology. Cotton knew Edison because "the boneman" as his students called him, ran a program that took young kids on trips to discover fossils. Cotton and Teddy had gone along, and Edison had developed a strong bond with the Down Syndrome child.

"Hey, man, how are you?" he asked as he spooned potato salad on his plate.

"Good, Edison. And yourself?"

"I'm fine. Judy couldn't come because someone had to take Jesse to soccer practice." He was a big man and had at one time been a serious power lifter. When he stopped, he slimmed down a bit, but he was still husky.

"How's my man, Teddy?" asked Edison.

There was a silence before Jen answered. "That's a sore spot," she said.

Edison frowned. "Is he ok?" he asked, concern in his voice.

"His mother is thinking of institutionalizing him," said Cotton.

"At his age? That's way too early," said Edison.

"I agree, but the father won't have anything to do with him and is using him a bargaining chip in their relationship. I got into an argument with my sister the other day and it got ugly. I came on too strong and I regretted it."

"If there's anything I can do, let me know. He's a great kid. And he likes bones which means he's way up there in my book."

They continued down the food line, adding on as they went.

"Whoa, pecan pie," said Cotton.

"I'm laying off that. I've already started my autumn diet."

"Autumn diet? What's that?" Cotton asked.

"A diet you start to make up for all the picnic food you ate during the summer!"

CHAPTER 26

The fall winds were kicking up all around the demonstrators who were out in full force the following Monday. Signs nailed to 2X4's, were waved at passers-bys. The whole scene was reminiscent of a street parade. Whenever they spied a student, they shouted for them to join the mob. If they didn't, they heckled them. Cotton was used to it.

"Hey, professor, come and join the line."

"Can't do it guys. Someone must work around here! "Cotton replied.

They picked up on the humor and egged him on.

"Working for the man. Isn't that, right?" a tall lanky red head said.

Cotton smiled. He had a good relationship with most of the students on the picket line. They knew him as a teacher who had an open door and would fight for a student if need be.

As he walked by the department office, Greta Aston, the history department secretary said in a casual voice, "Dr. Cunningham, your mail?"

This was a running joke between the two of them. Cotton never checked his mail and when it got to the point where it was overflowing, Greta would crack a remark that would embarrass Cotton. As usual, the mail was flowing out onto the floor.

"Wow, that's really a traffic jam, isn't it?" he remarked.

"That's an understatement," she said.

With a beehive hairdo and miniskirt, Greta was a spectacle and a formidable figure who could make life rough for anybody who got on her wrong side.

Most of Cotton's mail was junk – mail from publishers touting a new history book. There were also memos about meetings and committee work. Cotton was exempt from most of those because of his work for Meyerson. Most of this mail was heading for the circular file, but one flyer caught his eye.

> **Please help us celebrate the life of Dean Jillian Asbury in a memorial service in her memory this Saturday at 11:00 A.M. at St. Stephen's Episcopal Church, 44 Delaware Avenue, Buffalo New York**

There was an imperial crown on top of the page and filigree all around. It could have been put in the mailbox that day or last week.

"I got one in my mailbox also. I think someone's trying to drum up an audience," said Greta.

"Did you see who brought the flyers around?" asked Cotton.

"Yeah, a short stumpy guy in a blue works shirt stained with ink," she said.

Cotton immediately thought of the hanger-on, the fan, Bowers from the print shop. Another one to question. The list was widening.

"I think I might go. She seemed like an interesting person to me."

"A little aloof, if you ask me," said Greta.

"You knew her?" Cotton asked.

"Sure, we've been around a long time. I watched her come up the ladder. She stepped over a lot of bodies to get to be dean. I was never impressed. Beneath the veneer, there was a basic insecurity about her. I don't know how to put it, but she was a cold lady."

You're not the first person to say that," said Cotton.

"Well, it caught up to her in the end," said Greta, "didn't it? Suicide?"

"That's what the cops think," Cotton said as he headed for his office.

Chapter 27

The phone call started out in a controlled manner.

"He's been coming around and interviewing everyone."

"Of course, he has. He's been tasked by Meyerson to do that. He's come up with nothing and if we sing the same song, he never will."

"He's been at the beach house. He's got a picture of us."

"The picture proves nothing other than that you were all friends. After all, you taught together. If you panic, then there's trouble. It's what got Jillian into trouble. She had a change of heart. When the body was discovered, she went to pieces. Don't do the same thing."

"That's easy for you to say. I was her lover."

"She had many lovers. And many of those people would be exposed if she had faltered. Just repeat this to whoever questions you. You don't know anything about that boy or Jillian's death. Keep repeating that to yourself and you will be safe."

There was a long pause. "You didn't kill her, did you?"

The line went dead.

Chapter 28

Cotton drove down Jefferson Avenue, checking street addresses, looking for 615. As a policeman, he traveled down Jefferson many times. Domestic disputes, drive by shootings, young people with guns. Jefferson was a tough street for a cop.

On one occasion, he had a call about a domestic dispute. The husband had caught his wife with another man. The husband shot the man and was holding his wife at gunpoint. They put in a call for a hostage negotiator, but before he could get there, things turned bad. The dying man that was shot, stumbled into the kitchen, and grabbed the husband. The gun went off twice, killing the husband and a young child. The wife eventually committed suicide. A senseless waste.

The address was a run-down store front, with counter-culture posters in the window. "Free Huey" was the dominant theme. Cotton parked his car out front and walked to the door. A few teenagers were loitering on the steps of the house next door.

A bell rang when he entered. The bookstore smelled of smoke – pipe smoke, cigarette, and reefer. The inside of the store was ringed by makeshift bookshelves made by cement blocks and 2X8 pieces of lumber. A coffee table with chairs was center in front of the checkout counter.

A man dressed in a multicolored dashiki with a rimless cap on his head looked up from a chair with a mild expression of surprise.

"Don't get many white people coming round. You must lead a charmed life or else you a cop."

"Used to be," said Cotton. "Now I teach history at UB."

"My story is ancient history."

Cotton pulled out the picture he took off the refrigerator at Jillian Asbury's lake house and laid it on the counter. Ahmed Bhakta glanced at it. At first, there was no reaction, then a realization overcame him, and he slumped back in his chair.

"Where did you get this?" he whispered.

"Off Jillian Asbury's bulletin board in her summer house at Crystal Beach."

"Jillian Asbury's dead," he said, still not comprehending what was happening. "How did you come by it?"

"A buried body was discovered on the UB campus. It was identified as a student who disappeared back in 1948. Jillian Asbury died in what police called a suicide but what could be something else. I believe there's a connection. President Meyerson has asked me to investigate the matter. He thinks my previous job could make me an ideal person for the job."

Cotton was lying when he said this. Meyerson had explicitly ordered him off the case.

"How do you like teaching at UB?" Ahmed Bhakta asked.

"I like it," Cotton answered.

"Better watch your step then. When I started asking questions and doing things differently, they fired my ass."

"What questions did you ask?" said Cotton.

Bhakta reached around to one of the countertop

drawers and pulled out some rolling papers and a bag of what looked like marijuana. Very slowly and delicately, he rolled a joint.

"Questions like why a teacher who had fewer publications than me, who had less teaching experience and who avoided committee work like the plague, got tenure over me."

"Are you referring to Jillian Asbury?" Cotton asked.

He took a drag off the joint, held it in and slowly exhaled.

"Yes, I am," he said with an air of resignation.

"You looked like friends in the picture," said Cotton.

"That was before the tenure question," said Bhakta. "We used to hang out together at each other's apartments, party, and such. I think they included me because they thought it was cool to have a Black friend. Like I was a token. I was older than they were, shit, for some of them it was their first job. The older woman in the picture, I forget he name. We were in our thirties. I had taught at a community college before that and at UB for a couple of years."

"Did you get to know them well, the younger ones?" asked Cotton.

"Somewhat. They were a clique. Tight- lipped and moody. There weren't many brothers on campus in those days, so I took company wherever I could," said Bhakta.

"Do you remember when the student disappeared?" asked Cotton.

"Sure, it was a big deal on campus. We were all questioned about it, whether we knew him or taught him. I had no association with him," said Bhakta.

"How did the others feel about the disappearance?" asked Cotton.

He took another drag on the joint and then offered it to Cotton. Cotton declined.

"Strange you should ask. I remember Asbury being very shook up. She even took a few days off. I think she was his faculty advisor."

"Then she gained tenure over you," asked Cotton.

Bhakta was quiet for over a minute before he replied.

"Yes, she did. Under questionable circumstances. She had others who could speak up for her. Her references were good. Her friends lobbied for her. I did not have the connections and to make matters worse, I was a mentor to Black groups on campus, who were starting to question the establishment. When it came down to it, I had no pull. I complained, none too delicately and I was let go. I struggled after that, went homeless for a while. With the help of some friends, I got a job on the line at Bethlehem Steel. Made enough money to buy this building. I started this store and tried to give back to the community. The books were mostly academic to begin with and then I got into Black literature, then some radical stuff. A lot of Black college students started coming in from UB, Buffalo State and Canisius. They came here because they felt some things were changing. Remember that song by that long haired, skinny guy?"

"Yeah, Bob Dylan—*The Times They are a Changin*," said Cunningham.

"Well, It's sort of a community center of sorts. I make it comfortable to hang out. We sit around, drink coffee and talk about our experiences. I guess I'm a father confessor to some of them."

"Do you think that Jillian Asbury, or any of her friends, could have had anything to do with the disappearance of that boy back in 1948?" asked Cotton.

Bhakta seemed to be drifting away. Maybe it was the smoke or maybe it was the foul memories.

"I don't know if I would go that far," he said. "But they were a strange group of people, a lot of petty jealousies, insecurities and anger." His voice trailed off and he slumped back in his chair. A man trying to escape the past and failing.

Chapter 29

On Saturday, the day of the memorial service, Cotton got up early to grade papers. Getting a head start on the day, he was making progress when the phone rang.

"I'm calling to see if you're going to the service," said Drew.

"Yes, I am," said Cotton. "I think it will be an excellent way of seeing many of the suspects and how they act together."

"Suspects? Do you mean you have actual suspects or just people who knew Asbury?"

"Hell, Jefferson, they're as close as thieves and hiding something. That makes them suspects."

He related to Drew the conversation he had with Bhakta the day before.

"Did he give up anything useful?" asked Drew.

"He ran with that group for a while until he was denied tenure. He was pretty pissed over that. He feels that he was denied tenure for political reasons and that he was a better teacher than Asbury, but she had connections that a Black man didn't have."

"You showed me that picture with them at the beach," said Drew. "It was interesting that Davis was part of the group. There's quite an age difference."

"That wasn't lost on me," said Cotton. "When I interviewed her, she was very tight -lipped and formal. In fact, none of them were forthcoming."

"Yeah, well, I'm heading over to the memorial service. I'll see you there."

Cotton hung up and took his breakfast dishes to the sink. After cleaning up, he went to his bedroom and set out a semi-formal outfit befitting a somber occasion. Black sport coat, white shirt, neutral tie, and grey slacks with penny loafers. For school, Cotton was more of a sweater, button down shirt and khaki pants guy. The tweed sport coat with patches on the sleeves never appealed to him.

He could have walked to St Stephan's, but took his car instead. He had just acquired a 1962 Rambler with a standard transmission on the column. He had inspected a red 1965 Mustang convertible, but they weren't exactly winter vehicles. They were the rage and Cotton could dream.

On the way over, his mind raced through several possibilities. The most obvious was suicide, but Cotton believed that Barker caught Asbury stealing his intellectual property and Asbury had to kill him to protect herself. But still, that was a rather drastic move for an academic to be part of. Why didn't she just barter with Barker? Promise him a clear path to a doctorate if he would forget a slight indiscretion on her part? Or did she haggle, deny any wrongdoing, clam up so that it was just his word against her. No, she couldn't have done that because there was too much evidence that Barker had done the work. Did he have something else on her? Something more serious? What about the others? How were they involved? Could one of them be capable of murder?

St. Stephan's was a turn of the century monolith that spanned a whole city block. It fit in well with the stately mansions of a bygone era. The parking lot was full, and cars lined the avenue. Men in black suits and women in dark dresses with veils proceeded into the church. Cunningham parked down a side street and had a five-minute walk. Two police cars were parked in front with officers directing traffic.

While he approached the church, he spied President Meyerson entering the building. Other college officials, including department heads were present. Cotton wasn't sure who was delivering the eulogy, but circumstances around the death were such that Meyerson had declined the duty.

The church was large enough to hold the crowd with room to spare. Cotton favored a seat in the back where he could view all in attendance.

They came one by one, those who Cotton had interviewed and those who appeared in the photograph. Lisbeth Scott, dressed in a black, below the knee dress, that accented her figure- she was at least 5' 10"in Cotton's estimation.   She proceeded to a seat in front but off to the side. The rest of them scattered throughout the front of the church. They arrived separately and would no doubt leave the same way.

Cotton saw Bowers from the print department. He settled in the middle, away from the others. Cotton saw his chance and took it. He slid into the seat beside Bowers. When Bowers glanced to his side, he almost jumped into the air. Cotton nodded at him and tuned to face the front of the church. He could sense Bower's nervousness. There wasn't a moment of the service that he wasn't fidgeting, crossing, or uncrossing his knees and acting totally unsettled.

The memorial began with the minister, who seemed totally unfamiliar with Asbury, attempting to laud her with information that had obviously been funneled to him in a previous meeting with her friends. The chair of the Political Science department was next, and he carried on about her academic accomplishments before she became dean. Various other faculty spoke of her contributions on committees and her devotion to the college. Not one of them, Cotton noticed, said anything about her as a person, whether she loved dogs, donated any time to the Salvation Army or contributed to any worthwhile causes. None of the people who Cotton had interviewed spoke on her behalf. The service was brief and unemotional, and he had the feeling that most people wanted to be out as soon as possible.

When the service had concluded, Cotton turned to Bowers.

"How well did you know the Dean?"

Bowers stared at Cotton, muttered something unintelligible and ran out of the church.

Cotton tried to buttonhole other members of the group, but they escaped through various exits.

As he was leaving, a woman came up from behind and grabbed his arm. She was short with a page boy cut and puffy cheeks. She was dressed for the occasion with a short black dress that unfortunately did not hide her overweight figure.

"Dr. Cunningham, I'm Jillian Asbury's sister. We spoke on the phone. You were pointed out to me by President Meyerson."

Cotton recovered quickly. "Yes, please accept my sympathies."

Cotton noticed there were no swollen eyes, traces of grief or any other signs of emotion. Her tone was business like and perfunctory.

"I wonder if we could speak for a moment," she asked.

"Certainly," said Cotton. "Let's find a place outside away from the crowd."

They settled on a picnic bench down the street from the church.

She quickly came to the point. "I wonder if the police have made any headway in my sister's death?"

"The police are still looking at it as a suicide. That's one possibility," said Cotton.

"And there are others?" she asked.

"She was upset over the body that we found," said Cotton.

"That could lead to suicide, couldn't it?" she asked.

'Or it could be that there were several people involved and someone was afraid of what she knew," he said.

"Dr. Cunningham, you're making this out to be a conspiracy," she said.

"I don't mean for this to be pure conjecture on my part. I just believe that the police tend to accept the simplest explanation and suicide is the simplest."

"Well, in my opinion, you might be right," she said.

"Why's that?" Cotton asked.

"Because I can see someone wanting to kill her. There was a time when I would have."

COTTON was walking back to his car when a vehicle pulled over and the window rolled down.

"Well, what do you think?" asked Jefferson Drew. He was out of his sport coat with his tie hung loose.

"I jacked up Bowers a little. Sat next to him and he freaked out. He couldn't wait for it to end so he could leave. Just about jumped over a pew. I talked to Asbury's sister. What a sweetheart. She admitted that once upon a time, she could have done her in herself."

"Well, I'm headed back to campus. I got wind of a demonstration that YAWF plans to hold tonight in front of the library."

YAWF was Youth Against War and Fascism. They, along with the SDS, Students for a Democratic Society and various Black Power groups were a constant thorn in Drew's side. He had quit city police work for a quieter campus job and then realized that he wasn't catching any break. The Democratic National Convention in Chicago had ended with students being beaten in the street. Cotton knew that the campus was boiling over and the school year was in jeopardy.

He headed back to his apartment to grade papers, but his mind was on Bowers. He was a logical candidate to squeeze.

Chapter 30

Thornton Delaware had arrived at his house, a Victorian just off Main Street in Williamsville, when the phone rang. It was Bowers.

"What's wrong now," Delaware said with exasperation in his voice. He poured himself a drink. *Lord knows, "I deserved one, he thought."*

"He snuck up on me at the memorial. Sat next to me the whole time. I was sweating bullets. Then he starts to interrogate me, just like a common criminal."

"Calm down man. Get a hold of yourself," said Delaware. "He's got nothing on you."

There was a pause on the line.

"Paul? He has nothing on you, right?" Now Delaware's voice was rising.

"No, no, of course not," replied Bowers.

"Then anytime he confronts you, you deny, deny, deny. Listen, now I have no Idea who killed Barker or what happened to Asbury. As far as I'm concerned, she popped some pills, drank some booze, and went off to meet her maker."

"I'm glad you're so sure of yourself," said Bowers. "Some of us are on edge."

"Don't let them see you sweat, Paul," And he hung up.

Delaware sat down on his couch, cradling the gin and tonic in his hands. He wasn't sure about Paul. He was unstable, flying off the deep edge. In fact, he wasn't sure about any of them. He knew that Jillian had threatened to go public. Standing on her front porch that night, he had heard voices from within. He decided to come back later.

Chapter 31

Cotton was on the line with his sister. He had given her a week to simmer, but she was still angry.

"I'm sorry about what I said," he began. "I had no right to imply that you didn't care about Teddy. I know that you must be in a terrible position, and I called to offer any help that I can."

She was in tears now.

"No, you don't know. You don't know anything. You waltz in like a Good Time Charlie, take him for a few hours to places I could never take him, because I don't have the money and have other children to contend with and then you go back to your solitary existence."

Cotton kept his mouth shut. He knew anything he said would be useless.

In the end, Cotton took Teddy off her hands for a few hours. They drove around aimlessly, past gas stations, stores and finally ended up at the South Shore Plaza. They parked and Cotton took him into AM&A's, Adam Meldrum and Anderson's, an upscale department store. They didn't go in to buy clothes, they went into ride the escalator. Teddy loved the repetitive motion of the contraption. He giggled and fussed through the whole ordeal. The salesclerk smiled. They were familiar with Teddy. The store manager made sure that Teddy had a sample of chocolate from the candy aisle before he was through.

As they wandered back to the car, Cotton wondered about Teddy's future. There weren't many possibilities. If Teddy's parents decided to institutionalize him, there was nothing that Cotton could do. His only option was to try to convince them to keep him at home, but Cotton's sister had said that would ruin their marriage. Maybe Cotton could provide financial aid. He could talk to Fred about it. Arrange for babysitters to give them a break. He could keep Teddy for the weekends. *"Goodbye relationship with Jen, he thought."* He dropped Teddy back at his house without as much as a word to his sister who met him with a cold stare.

Chapter 32

Cotton was in his office putting together a lecture on the Constitution. He had pulled down at least three books to examine. Was the Constitution a compact with the devil as William Lloyd Garrison once said? He was tossing this question around in his mind when a call came in from President Meyerson's office.

"Cunningham, I was asked too many hard questions about Asbury at the memorial service the other day. People from high up in Albany in State ED and even the governors' office. They want to know the circumstances of her death. If it was a suicide, then they want to know why we didn't monitor the situation better. If it wasn't a suicide, I hate to think of the scandal involved in a violent death. What have you got for me?"

"I can't rule out suicide, but I'm still troubled by other circumstances."

"Cotton, we've gone over this before. Don't overthink this. A suicide is messy, but a murder is catastrophic."

"I hear you. I can't promise this will be wrapped up in a nice, neat bow," said Cotton.

"I'll repeat what I told you before. Investigate, but watch who you implicate. We have a college to think about."

CHAZ Barker's brother called soon after.

"Did you get the package?" he asked.

"Yes, I did, thank you," said Cotton.

"Did you find anything out when you read through the material?" he asked.

Cotton paused. He started to rethink his policy of sharing suppositions with civilians.

Chaz's brother read into the pause. "I know it! You found something. What was it?" he demanded.

"I can't share anything with you now. I'm not done going through the papers, but I can tell you that the relationship between your brother and the dean was acrimonious."

Ned Barker laughed. "I knew that from the beginning. He complained to me about her more than once. She was a hindrance."

"Ned, I know that you want closure on your brother's death after all these years and if you give me enough time, I'll think you'll get it," said Cotton.

'All right, I guess I have no choice. And by the way, I remembered something that may be relevant. Before, he was murdered, he mentioned that he had something on Asbury."

Cotton perked up. "What do you mean he had something?"

"It was like there was something in her past or something she was doing that he could hold over her. Like he caught her in the act. He wouldn't get any more explicit than that."

Cotton was silent for a moment. "If you can remember anything more about that, please let me know. It could be very important."

"Yeah, sure. And if you find out anything more, please contact me."

Cotton swiveled around in his office chair and faced the window looking out over the courtyard. How did this new information bear upon the case.? Was Chaz blackmailing Asbury? Was it the thesis or something else? If it was something else besides the thesis, then murder could be the answer. She killed Chaz to keep him from revealing something in her past. She was consumed by guilt and committed suicide. The police would buy that. They liked things simple. But a dean and murder? Meyerson would hate it. Meyerson would never hide the truth. He was an honest person. The public perception of the University would take a hit. But to Cotton, it was the truth that mattered. It always was.

CHAPTER 33

It was a lazy Sunday at Jen's walk up in Allentown. They were lounging around reading newspapers after scrambled eggs and bagels. Jen's apartment was a tad more thought out than Cotton's bachelor digs. Framed photos of international travel lined the walls interspersed with watercolors from prominent local artists. Dried flower arrangements and hanging plants led a hint of nature to the surroundings. Bookcases lined the living room walls and a burnt orange shag carpet lay between two couches that faced each other. It was an open arrangement with kitchen and living room flowing seamlessly into one another. Cotton's favorite piece of furniture was a waterbed on the second floor.

Cotton was reading the sports section of the Courier Express, while Jen was paging through the New York Times Review of Books.

"That was quite a game last weekend," said Cotton. The Buffalo Bills started a young, rookie quarterback named Dan Darragh from William and Mary. Even though Darragh threw for only eighty yards, the Bills defeated the New York Jets 37-35. They won because of Joe Namath's horrible performance. He threw five interceptions with three of those being returned for touchdowns.

"Ugh," said Jen. She had received both her undergraduate and graduate degrees from Columbia and was a diehard Jet's fan. That allegiance extended to both the Yankees and the Knicks.

"It was ugly, but I still think the Jets are going places this year," she said.

They continued to page through the news.

"How about this name for a book? *The Electric Kool-Aid Acid Test*" said Cotton.

"Is that the book about Ken Kesey and his merry pranksters?" said Jen.

"Ken Kesey, yes, that's the one," said Cotton.

They were lying on opposite ends of the couch, with their legs intertwined. *God,* thought Cotton. *If this was what domestic life was about, then I'm all for it.*

"Jen, remember when we talked about moving in together?"

"Yes, "she said.

"Have you thought about it anymore?" he asked.

Jen put down the newspaper. "Sure. And I thought about pluses and minuses."

"Such as?" asked Cotton.

"On the minus side there's the loss of autonomy. Look around you. Everything here is me. The books, the floor plan, the décor. It's all thought out and deliberate."

"So, you're saying that intimacy is a threat to autonomy?" asked Cotton.

"Very well put, Cotton. Your argument is thought out," she said.

"It's not an argument, Jen. It's a question," Cotton said.

"A question that's been tossed around for a millennium, Cotton, with no real answer. You can't generalize. It depends, I think it depends on how mature and adaptable people are."

"Well, I think we're both mature and I would hope we both are adaptable. Autonomy doesn't necessarily mean that I want to decide on the colors of the living room or whether we have wall to wall carpeting rather than area rugs. It means allowing each other to be individuals. The freedom to choose how to act in any given situation."

"Of course. Are you worried that you would give that up if we moved in together?" she asked.

"I wouldn't last long in a relationship if that happened," he laughed. "I just think that if we moved in together, there's a certain amount of compromise involved. I'm not the kind of person who's obsessive over the house colors or which side of the bed I get out of. I'm more concerned with my ability to come and go as I please." He paused. "Before we get into that, let me state that I think we could work our way out of that. I'm in favor of the intimacy part."

"I'm concerned about all those things that you brought up. And by the way, I'm not obsessive."

"No? How about when you fold the toilet paper over and make the pointy things like they do in the motels?"

The sports section barely missed his head.

Chapter 34

Dolores Davis was lounging on one her the plush leather couches when she took the phone call. It was a Sunday afternoon and not the day that she wanted to be distracted from leisure pursuits.

"Delores, this is Elsbeth."

Davis had been expecting the call ever since ever since Cunningham had been roaming around, trying to trip up people.

"Elsbeth, what's on your mind?"

Elsbeth had always been wary of Davis. Delores was a control freak. She was domineering and demanded to have her way. And she had a mean streak.

"Cunningham is snooping around interviewing people. He's trying to draw connections between us and Barker. My relationship with Jillian makes me a suspect."

"Yes, you were quite the fox back then, weren't you? How many did you bed down in those days, Elsbeth? Boys and girls alike. You weren't very picky, were you?"

"Cut the crap, Delores. You have a few dark secrets too, don't you? But that doesn't matter right now. What matters is that secrets stay secrets. The fact of the matter is that I don't have any idea who murdered the boy or how Jillian died."

Delores smiled into the phone. *You know more than you're saying,* she thought.

"Elsbeth, he has nothing on any of us. Unless, of course, someone breaks. Stay the course, girl."

Chapter 35

otton's father was dying, and it was a slow death. His organs were failing. It was a cumulation of fifty years of drinking, poor diet and lack of any exercise other than cheating on his wife.

Cotton didn't know what he felt. Part of him just wanted it to go away. He knew he had to be honest with his father, talk to him about things he always wanted to say but avoided. Ever since his father had entered the nursing home, Cotton had done the bare minimum. He visited every few weeks, made sure that he had the basics, keeping up his ends of conversations with one-word answers. Often, he left after a short time, sick of his father's banter about the good old days, Cotton's career mistakes and what a burden Teddy was. He wanted to talk about Cotton's days on the force. He reveled in the violence.

The worst thing of all is that he wanted Cotton to be his buddy, a drinking pal who would curse, make derogatory comments about women, spew racist epithets, and talk about what a man he was.

What Cotton saw was pitiful old man, who stayed in his pajamas all day long and could barely keep his head up.

Cotton was angry, but he didn't want to take out his anger on a dying man.

"Cotton, remember when you worked at the steel

plant during the summer, and we would go out after the shift and have a few beers with the guys? That was a grand time!"

Cotton remembered. He remembered having a few beers and having to drag his father out of the bar and drive him home. Most of the time, if his mother wasn't laid up with a migraine, there was a decent meal on the table which his father gobbled up and then headed for the recliner. The rest of the evening was a baseball game or a boxing match on the radio before he would fall asleep in a stupor.

That's the bonding he remembered.

"How are the kids doing?" his father asked.

"Fine, dad." He didn't mention the situation with Teddy. His father had long ago labeled Teddy as a burden to the family. He would undoubtedly agree with the attempt to institutionalize him.

Cotton's father rambled on for quite a long time until he was finally silent.

Cotton looked down at his father and noticed a tear running down his cheek.

"Cotton, I'm afraid of dying," he said.

Cotton was taken aback. He didn't know what to do.

"I know, Dad, I know," he said. He reached down to hold his father's hand. He held it long into the night.

Chapter 36

He was in his one o'clock American History class the next day taking attendance when Jimmy Salukis slid into a seat in the rear of the lecture hall. Cotton did a double take when he saw that Salukis was bruised over his face with a mouse underneath his right eye. Cotton continued with the class and when it was done, signaled to Jimmy to meet with him. They waited until the classroom emptied,

"Well," said Cotton, "I've seen you looking better."

"Yeah," said Salukis. "I'd like to say you should have seen the other guy, but there were two of them."

"Yeah, those godless Commies tend to run in packs," said Cotton.

Jimmy started to laugh but stopped in obvious pain.

"No jokes, man. It hurts like hell."

"Sorry, Jimmy. Tell me what happened."

Jimmy slumped down into a chair.

"I was walking across campus last night. I have a six thirty class with Henderson in Sociology. There was a bunch of protesters. A couple of them broke ranks and came over to me. They asked me why I wouldn't join them. I tried to explain why when one of them cold cocked me from behind. I hit the ground rolled over and got back up. By then, there were more than two. They crushed me. Then security arrived and the crowd dispersed. Security asked me if I wanted to go to the hospital, but I begged off. It's not as bad as it looks."

"Look, man, I can talk with a few people about this. Part of my job is to act as a bridge between students and administration. This sort of thing should not go on at a college campus. I know a lot of these protesters. I could talk with them."

"Dr. Cunningham, I don't want you to fight my battles. It just helps talking to someone who served."

Jimmy stopped and collected himself. He didn't want to lose control in front of Cotton.

"I just want to be left alone to take classes, study, get a degree and a job. I want to get on with my life, leave that damn war behind."

"Jimmy, I'm sorry about what happened to you. We need to get the veteran's group on campus to talk with the leaders of the protest movement. It would be a start."

"As long as you leave me out of this. I don't want to be known as a whiner. I can fight my own battles," Jimmy said.

"Yeah and how's that going?" asked Cotton.

Jimmy laughed and doubled over with pain.

Chapter 37

Cotton met Cassandra Day for lunch at her house in East Amherst. It was a large Tudor edifice that Cassandra had lived in since the late thirties. The lawns were manicured with rose bushes lining the long curving driveway. Cotton counted seven large maple trees in the front yard. Side paths led to the backyard where Cassandra had laid out a sumptuous spread on a wrought -iron table set on a brick patio. There was fruit, vegetables with dip and different slices of bread with luncheon meat.

"Cassandra, I didn't mean for you to go to all this trouble when I asked to meet."

"Cotton, I rarely do this anymore. I remember years when the University used my backyard for parties to welcome new faculty. These days, it's only for bridge parties in late summer and early fall. I rarely have company anymore."

They spent a minute loading their plates. Cotton noticed the small amount of food on her plate.

"That's not enough to feed a mouse," said Cotton.

"I have to work to keep my figure as I get older," she remarked with a smile.

"Do you still get on the golf course? "asked Cotton.

She brightened. "Of course. That is one of the few passions in my life that I still indulge in."

Cotton remembered that in the fifties and early sixties, Cassandra was one of the leading amateur female golfers in Western New York. He had golfed with her and was amazed that such a slight person could drive a golf ball so far.

After exchanging a few more pleasantries, he got down to business.

"I know we've gone over this before, but I would like you to think back over the time in 1948 when Chaz Barker disappeared. I am thinking of a few people, Lisbeth Scott, Thornton Delaware, Dolores Davis, and Donald Bowers. What do you remember of them back then?"

"Cotton, that's twenty years ago. Most of them were students, I believe."

"Do your best, Cassandra. How about Scott?"

"I remember when she started, but I can't remember the year. She was quite the looker, still is. She was quiet as most beginning instructors are. Over the years, she's become more outspoken, almost imperious. I remember her and Delaware hanging out at parties and faculty gatherings."

"How about Delaware?"

"He fits into the old-time male professor mold, smoking a pipe, always shirt, tie, and jacket. He is sociable enough. He works on committees and contributes at faculty meetings. As a teacher, I have no idea."

"Donald Bowers?"

"I have no idea who he is," she said.

"He works in the print shop," said Cotton.

"I would have very little reason to associate with him," said Cassandra.

"Dolores Davis?"

"Of course, I know Dolores. I have known her for decades. Even though, we are in different disciplines, we've served on panels, gone to faculty parties and even out of town workshops. I can't say that she's a friend. She's more an associate.

"What about Jillian?"

"Well Jillian was, in my estimation, a serviceable dean. I can't think of anything out of the ordinary, that she proposed or developed. I'm not on campus much anymore, even though I've kept my old office. I'm sorry I can't help you."

"Don't worry, Cassandra. Any information contributes to the picture," said Cotton.

"What are you going to do now?" asked Day.

"I'm not sure. Probably go back to some of the people we've discussed. Try to shake them up a little. Bowers seems like a person who might crack. I might go back to Acton Powers. By the way, his name is Ahmed Bhaktu now. And that picture is still bothering me."

She paused for a second.

"What does Meyerson think?" she asked.

"The President wants the problem settled and hopes the University can come out undamaged."

"Meyerson is a political animal, of course. He's thinking of the students, alumni and doners."

"I'm sure he does. He also wants to get to the truth," Cotton said.

"Well, I think you will find, Cotton Cunningham, that the truth, like History, is often muddled."

Chapter 38

Cotton decided to show up at the print shop unannounced. He wanted to catch Bowers by surprise. He was sure he could shake him up a bit. He seemed breakable.

The print shop consisted of two large rooms connected by a door in the middle. Bowers was in the first room dressed in jeans and a work shirt, his sleeves rolled up and his hands splattered with ink. As soon as he saw Cunningham, he looked around him, almost like he was checking escape routes and then he backed into a wall.

"Do you have a second?" asked Cotton.

At first, he stood there without answering. Then he muttered something under his breath.

"I'm sorry. I didn't catch that," Cotton said.

"I'm busy. I have a job that needs to go out immediately. I have no time to talk."

"Well then, perhaps we can arrange a time. I think the President would like to sit in also," Cotton said.

"No!" he screamed. "What do you want with me?"

"Just a few questions. How well did you know Jillian Asbury?"

"I knew who she was, but I never met her," he said cautiously.

"Then how do explain this picture?" asked Cotton. He laid it on the desk in front of Bowers.

Bowers glanced down at it and turned red.

"Don't fuck with me man! Don't fuck with me!" he screamed.

"The door to the adjoining room opened and a bushy haired man with tattoos leaned in.

"Do we have a problem here?" he asked.

"No problem. I was just leaving," said Cotton.

He moved to the door, but before he left, he turned around to Bowers.

"I'll be seeing you again, very soon," he said.

Chapter 39

Cotton had arranged to meet Fred at a small nondescript coffee house on main street in Williamsville. It was late in the afternoon and the hippies hadn't laid claim to place yet. The owner, with droopy pants and a ponytail tied back in a rubber band, was sweeping the floor. The place smelled of cigarette smoke and coffee grounds.

Even though he was only in his mid-thirties, Fred was beginning to show the signs of middle age. He was thickening around the waist and what was more concerning to Cotton, he had red veins coursing through his face – a sign of heavy drinking. He reminded Cotton of his own father during his younger years. Had his sister married a carbon copy of her father? His hair was already receding and showing signs of grey. Surprisingly, he met Cotton with a smile and a hearty handshake.

"Cotton, my man. It's been a long time. It's too bad we didn't meet at a bar. We could have downed a couple of brews and reminisced," he said.

That's just why Cotton had asked to meet at the coffee house. He had a feeling that Fred was a liquor salesman who sampled his own wares. He had nothing to reminisce about with him.

Cotton got right to the point. "I thought we could talk about Teddy and work out some solutions to the problem."

Fred's demeanor quickly changed.

"Cotton, Teddy is the problem. If we would have

known before, he was born, that he was retarded, I would have voted for an abortion. That would have been the solution right there."

Cotton bristled but he tried not to show it. "Fred, He's a great kid. Whenever I take him out, we have a wonderful time. He loves his home, his sisters, and his mother. He's happy there."

Fred frowned. "Cotton, you only have him for short periods of time. My wife has him all day. By the time I get home at night, she's exhausted. She has no time for me. You know, no time for me to get a little…"

He stopped right there, realizing that he was talking about Cotton's sister.

"Cotton, he's not good for our marriage. You have no idea what a burden he is. Frankly, on most days, I don't want to go home. You don't know how it feels, to be a stranger in your own home."

Cotton was trying to contain himself. *You wouldn't be such a stranger if you came home at a decent hour and helped her out. Then she wouldn't be so exhausted at the end of the day,* he thought.

"Fred, I'm sure if we brainstormed, tried to figure out a way to ease the burden on both of you, we could keep Teddy where he belongs," Cotton said.

"That's just it, Cotton. An institution is where he belongs. He doesn't belong with us. He belongs with other retards, with his own kind. Where people can take care of him, teach him some skills."

"Fred, he's too young. There's time for that when he's older," Cotton said.

"Cotton, it's either Teddy or my marriage. That's the deal."

Cotton left the coffee house before his order came.

Chapter 40

Cotton was sitting in his office watching students scurrying to escape the torrential downpour that had erupted over the campus. He had just closed his window when he received a phone call from Jefferson Drew.

"Cotton, something strange is going on. Remember when you told me you braced that Bowers fellow at the memorial service for Asbury. Have you seen him lately?"

"Yes, I have. I went to the print shop last Friday and confronted him about that picture I found at Asbury's summer home."

"How did he take that?" asked Drew.

"He completely freaked out," said Cotton. "Started swearing up a blue streak. Why do you ask?"

"He hasn't been to work for a couple days. And he hasn't called in. They say that's very unusual because he never misses any time. He's not answering his phone. One of his friends from the print shop cruised by his house and saw his car there. He rang the doorbell, but he got no answer. Then they called me because they didn't know what to do. I called up the Buffalo Police and they said there was not much they could do until a missing person's report was filed."

"Usually that's between 24-72 hours unless there are dire circumstances. We need to get into his house. Where does he live?" asked Cotton.

"Near Canisius College by Forest Lawn Cemetery, "answered Drew.

"I can call up some people I know on the Buffalo Police force and explain the situation. I can say that he was in a distraught state the last time he was seen, and we suspect something serious. I think they'll enter the house under those conditions."

"OK," said Drew. "Let me know what you come up with."

Cotton made the requisite calls and later that day the police entered the home, and they found an empty house. Cotton requested permission to search the house and with Meyerson's intersession they received permission, but only if a Buffalo policeman was present.

THE next morning, Cotton, Jefferson Drew and Officer Jack Davis entered the house. What they saw mirrored Bower's personality.

Blinds were drawn tight with just slivers of natural light floating through. Dust motes meandered in the air in a house that Cotton doubted ever saw a deep cleaning. There were no pictures on the walls, no plants, nothing to give a clue to the occupant's personality. The kitchen was decorated in early Chinese take-out, with flies taking occupancy. The furniture was old and worn. Jackets and clothes were scattered everywhere. Bowers obviously did little entertaining.

The dining room table was cluttered with boxes carrying material from the print shop. It was clear that Bowers never ate there, preferring to dine on a series of director's chairs that faced a small black and white television that was perched precariously on a small table.

A search of the upstairs revealed two bedrooms, one with boxes piled high, perhaps from a previous move. The other bedroom contained box springs and mattress on the floor and the bed. An alarm clock and a collection of pornographic magazines lay on the floor next to the bed. A closet contained shirts and pants, some of which had fallen off their hangers lay on the floor below. A small dresser with drawers half open contained underwear, socks, and gym shorts.

The upstairs bathroom contained a shower with a curtain that was stained green. The tub had not been scrubbed in a millennium. The medicine cabinet contained a hairbrush an open tube of toothpaste, aspirin, tweezers, fingernail clippers and bottles of medicine, one of which Cotton recognized as a anti-depressant.

Nothing in the house, however, indicated a struggle of any kind or any evidence of a forced entry. Bowers had left, with no evidence of whether he was forced to leave or had left of his own free will.

Jillian Asbury and now Bowers. The suspect list was growing smaller.

Chapter 41

Cunningham was in his office gazing out his window. It was early in the morning and the campus was strangely deserted. It was like all the eight o'clock classes had been cancelled and the students were still fast asleep. The only sounds from outside his office was a janitor's push broom. The phone rang. It was Meyerson. Cotton could read the frustration in his voice.

"Cunningham, are you sure that the disappearance of this Bowers fellow is connected to the suicide of Asbury?"

"I think so, sir. Bowers, Asbury, Scott, and Delaware were tight over the years. To think his disappearance is an isolated incident is too much of a coincidence."

"Cunningham, this story is developing legs and I don't like it," said Meyerson.

"Yes, sir, I know. I am working to find some answers. I need time," said Cunningham.

"I've already informed the press that Asbury died by her own hand due to job pressures. That satisfied them, but Albany wants to know why we didn't see this coming. I mentioned to them about the death of her parents and how close they were."

Cunningham laughed. "Did you know the exact opposite was true? She was only interested in the estate and left her sister in the lurch. She was probably embarrassed by her parents."

"I was just throwing a bone to Albany to get them off my back. When or if this all comes out, it is going to be a publicity nightmare," Meyerson said. "Take all the time you need. Cancel classes if necessary. Get it done and done quickly!"

Meyerson slammed the phone.

Chapter 42

Cotton was having a cup of coffee at his kitchen table, reading the Courier Express when a story caught his eye.

A fire occurred at 615 Jefferson Avenue early this past morning, at the business residence of Ahmed Bhakta. Bhakta, whose residence was above the store, sustained critical burns in the fire and remains unresponsive in Intensive care now. The cause of the fire is unknown.

Cotton reread the blurb. A person who he had just spoke with weeks before was now unresponsive in intensive care. He had to find out more information.

He called up the Buffalo Police Department and asked for Chip Tully. They transferred him over immediately.

"Tully here," a gravelly voice answered.

"Chip, this is Cotton Cunningham. How are you?"

"Cunningham, I haven't heard from you since we had some brews over at Ulrich's," he said. "What was that 5-6 years ago? And now you spring up out of the blue. What's up Cotton?"

Chip Tully worked a lot of arson cases for the department and was very knowledgeable.

"Chip, that fire over on Jefferson Avenue last night.

Do you know anything more than what was in the paper this morning?"

"Oh yeah, I was there and right now I'm working on two or three hours of sleep," he said.

"Do you suspect Arson, Chip?" Cotton asked.

There was a pause on the phone. "Cotton, what do you know that we don't know?" Tully asked.

"Not much Chip. I know the guy. I just talked to him a few weeks ago. He was worried about some young kids in the area who had it out for him." Cotton was lying. He didn't want to explain any connection to what was going on at UB.

"Well, I examined the scene. We ruled out the common causes -faulty wiring, a cigarette butt. What I found out was something strange."

"How so?" Cotton asked.

"Well, some of the old timers clued me in on this a long time ago. They said that they had seen it during the twenties. It looked like a Molotov cocktail."

"Really?" asked Cotton.

"Yup," said Tully. "It was arson and considering that the guy was living upstairs, it was probably attempted murder."

Chapter 43

The next day Cotton was driving to work thinking about the fire. Stores spun by him as he drove down Main Street. Hardware stores, dry cleaners, mom-and-pop grocery stores, but none of them registered on Cotton's consciousness.

Cotton knew that he couldn't tell Meyerson. At least not yet. Meyerson would probably jump out of his window. Things were moving fast, and Cotton had to move with them. Bowers was missing. He had either fled because the pressure was building, or someone had eliminated him. If he fled, why hadn't he taken anything with him? His suitcase was still in his closet and toiletries were still in the medicine cabinet. His car was still in the driveway. Cotton needed to check with the police about any recent bank withdrawals. It would seem strange that he would flee without any of these things.

And Bhakta, what about him? Why would someone deem him a threat?

Bhakta was part of the group twenty years before but had not had any contact with the group since then. But Cotton had. There must be something about his visit to Bhakta that had caused the assault. And a Molotov cocktail? Who would use that? Certainly not your run of the mill academic. He thought back. Who knew that he was in contact with Bhakta? He had shown the picture to more than one person. Cotton felt very uneasy. He was used to being proactive. Now he was sitting back and letting events happen. He had to shake things up. He had to think back. How would he have handled this as a detective? He had to stop being a teacher and start being a cop. And that scared him.

Chapter 44

Cotton was at the print shop talking to Julius Carter, one of the print assistants and Bowers closest associate.

"Yeah, we used to go out and have a few beers together. He was not one to open up about his personal life. I don't know anything about his parents, brothers, and sisters, although I think he mentioned once about being an only child. We talked sports, what was happening at work and occasionally politics."

"Did he say or do anything in the few days leading up to his disappearance that could shed some light on his actions?" asked Cotton.

Carter was a big man, not in height but in circumference. If he would have to guess, Cotton would have said that he had done some heavy weightlifting in the past. The tattoos on his arms led Cotton to infer that gang associations had been part of his life. Cotton was aware of this from his time as a detective. Carter had lost most of his hair and what little that was left was pulled back in a ponytail. He had a freckled face and a perpetual grimace. Cotton could tell that he wasn't enjoying being questioned.

"He was plenty nervous in the days before he split and seeing you didn't help any. Man, he was so upset, he was shaking. He had to go home early. He came back the next day, but he wasn't the same. He was talking to himself while he was working, and it wasn't about no print shop job."

"Did you catch anything that he said?" asked Cotton.

"Not much, but he was swearing, and he did mention your name, Cunningham, right?"

"Yeah, that's me. Nothing else that you can recall?" asked Cotton.

"Nope, and then he just didn't show up," said Carter. He paused. "I gotta get back to work. The whole thing was fucking strange, you know what I mean?"

Cotton debated whether he should drive by Bhakta's House to see if the remains would give him a clue, but he decided against that. He needed to clear his mind and he knew just what to do to have that happen.

Chapter 45

Cotton owed Jen a night out and that didn't mean a meatloaf dinner at a mom-and-pop hash house. Jen was hoping something lavish, and Cotton wanted to impress. They settled on The Cloister, probably the most opulent restaurant in town. Built on the original site where Mark Twain lived, on the corner of Virginia and Delaware Avenues, the owners Jim and Angel DiLapo spared no expense in setting the atmosphere of the late 19th century. A Tiffany chandelier, some five feet in length, hung over the bar. Beside it was a mannequin, a woman, decked out in turn of the century apparel sitting in a swing. For seating you could opt for the Crystal Dining Room, the Green House or the Carriage House, each one replete with more Tiffany chandeliers and a wide assortment of plants. If you were there on the right night, you could hear Jackie Jocko on piano accompanied by Joey Peters on drums. It was the right night.

They had drinks at the bar, as they waited to be seated. The Hurricanes were a favorite drink of the day. Most of the conversation that they had of late centered on three topics—the case that Cotton was working on for the college, the delicate topic of their future living situation and academic happenings.

Cotton unloaded first. "I need to make things happen. I feel like I'm standing around just watching this story unfold without being part of it."

132

Jen sipped at her drink before replying. "How about this Bhakta fellow? Can you find out anything from him?"

"He's in intensive care at Buffalo General in an induced coma. They can't give me any indication of when he will be fit to talk. Bowers is missing with no clues on what happened. "

After a while, they were led to their table in the Green House. They ordered—Cotton got the prime rib, baked potato with green beans while Jen opted for something called Angel's Flounder—flounder stuffed with steamed crabmeat.

"It seems that you're at a standstill. How about reinterviewing people?" asked Jen.

"Scott and Delaware are the only ones left and I must be careful that I'm not setting myself up for a harassment charge. It's not like when I was a detective and we used to pull low lifes off the street to grill. These people are professionals in positions of prestige with no criminal records."

Their meals had arrived, and Cotton had ordered a Heineken with Jen still sipping on her Hurricane.

"It seems like the disappearance of Bowers and the arson are the key. If you can find out why these things happened, that will lead you to the answer. "

"Easier said than done," said Cotton. He wasn't too disappointed. He had a lovely evening to look forward to and more to come.

Chapter 46

Of course, other things interfered with his investigations. He had arranged a meeting with the veteran's group on campus and leaders of SDS, Students for a Democratic Society and YAWF, Youth Against War and Fascism. The meeting room was small and congested and that didn't lend itself to an amicable discussion. Cotton had only a casual acquittance with the students from both groups, but he knew Rick Larson well. Rick was head of the office of Veterans Affairs at the University. Jimmy Salukis declined an invitation to attend, but there were two veterans in attendance.

The protest groups took the offensive right away.

"We have the right to protest, and we oppose the presence of ROTC on campus. We try to put as much pressure as we can to get the administration to listen. The additional presence of Project Themis on campus is an example of the University collaborating with a government that is waging an unjust war."

Cotton saw himself as a facilitator in this meeting. He knew Harry Carlson from SDS. Cotton had Harry in more than one history class and found him to be reasonable but quick to anger.

"Harry, no one is disputing your right to protest on campus, but there have been instances of protesters harassing students, some of them veterans. Many of these people agree with some of your arguments, but don't want to get involved in demonstrations."

One of the veterans—Cotton didn't know his name—spoke up.

"While walking to class, I have been stopped by protesters who have asked me to join their picket lines. When I refuse, they get physical. There's pushing and shoving and more."

"Our veterans, who have fought for their country, just want the right to get an education. I think they deserve that courtesy," said Rick Larson.

"I do not encourage any of our protesters to physically prevent veterans or any other students from peacefully walking to classes. Like any organization, we have hot heads who cross over the line. I discourage these actions," said Harry.

"Maybe you should do more than discourage them. Maybe you should kick their asses off the line. We have fought for our country and if we must, we'll fight for a chance at an education," said the veteran.

Carlson bristled at this. "We have numbers on our side. Just because we didn't fight in Viet Nam, doesn't mean we won't fight to keep our campus free from oppression."

Cotton could see the discussion drifting towards a physical confrontation.

"Guys, no one wants this to escalate into violence. Both sides have rights here and I don't see them as conflicting. Harry, if you can convince some of your people to respect the rights of students, I think we can come to a peaceful solution."

The conversation continued for a half hour with both

slides slinging accusations at each other. In the end, Harry promised to talk to some of the more zealous protesters. Cotton thought some progress had been made, but there were still significant issues that defined both sides.

Chapter 47

The phone conversation was brief and to the point.

"Where is Bowers?"

"I have no idea. I know that Cunningham had been harassing him at work. You know Bowers, he can't stand the pressure."

"Did he leave town?"

"His car is still at his house."

"He wasn't involved with Jillian's death. Why would he feel pressured?"

"He's been involved since the beginning."

"What do you mean."

'We've all had a hand in it. Maybe we didn't pull the trigger, but we saw it coming."

COTTON was in his office, late at night when he received the call.

"Mr. Cunningham, this is the Bartholomew Home for the Aged. We have an emergency with you father. His heart stopped beating, but we've revived him. His vitals are all over the chart. We think you better get here as soon as possible."

Cotton hung up and dashed out the door. He took the stairs two at a time and was out in the parking lot in less than a minute. He jumped into his car and headed out in the parking lot heedless of the stop signs. It was past 10:00

and the traffic was scarce. He took the entrance ramp on the expressway way too fast. He was going sixty when he exited ten minutes later and felt the brakes go. He struggled to control the car, but he was still going forty when he flew through the stop sign at the bottom of the ramp, shot off the road, and flipped. The last thing he saw was the bent guardrail.

Chapter 48

When he woke up, he was staring at Jen Valley and Jefferson Drew.

Cotton looked around. A hospital room and a window with a view of a brick wall. He was hooked up to an IV, probably just fluids, a small table with his watch and a bucket to pee in.

"What do you remember?" asked Drew.

"Just like a cop," said Jen. "How do you feel?"

"Buffalo General?" Cotton asked.

"No, ECMC. It was closer," said Drew.

Cotton looked at Jen. "My neck feels like it's in a vice. My knee aches like the devil and I have a splitting headache."

"If that's all it is, you're lucky. You went through a guard rail and flipped over, landed upright," said Drew.

Cotton thought for a moment. Even that hurt.

"How's my dad?" Cotton asked.

"Your dad? Why do you ask?" said Jen.

"That's where I was headed, when I blacked out," said Cotton.

"Why do you think there's anything wrong with him?" asked Drew.

Cotton thought again. It was getting better. "I got a call that he was dying,"

Drew was silent for a moment. "We can check that

out, but right away, without checking, I would say that the call wasn't from your father's nursing home. I would bet that someone wanted you on your way in a hurry."

"Why?" asked Cotton.

"Because your break line was severed," Drew said. "The police had it checked when they towed your car in. Someone has it in for you."

"I think I'll be able to pay you back for all the time that you spent with me after my accident last year," said Jen with half a smile.

"What time is it?" Cotton asked.

Ten o'clock in the morning," said Drew." You slept peacefully through the night. Compliments of the hospital staff."

"Have they said when I can get out of her?" asked Cotton.

"They're talking tomorrow morning at the latest," said Jen. "I brought some class work for you to do and a few books. You should take it easy. They said it could have been much worse."

"This is unraveling faster than I thought. They're tying up loose ends," said Cotton with a grimace. "Bowers, Bhakta and me."

"Looks like it," said Drew.

"Cutting brake lines, Molotov cocktails, it sounds like the mob," said Cotton.

"Or someone very serious. Someone who has a lot to hide," said Drew.

Cotton convinced his doctor to be released later that day with the promise that Valley would stay with him.

"Straight home to bed with very little activity for the

next few days. You got shaken up bad. You have a slight concussion. You should be good to go in a few days."

They ended up at Cotton's apartment by nightfall. Cotton fell asleep on the ride home. She helped him to bed and then attended to some class work of her own.

The next day, against Valley's objections, he showered, dressed, and had her drive him into work. He lasted until noon before he had to call it a day. Valley drove him home and he settled onto the coach to think things over.

Meyerson called while they were dining on breakfast food.

"Cotton, how do you feel?" he asked.

"Better than yesterday," he said. "I should be back at school full time tomorrow."

"Cotton, you are now officially off this assignment. Stick to the classroom from now on," Meyerson said.

"I'll take your advice for a while, sir," said Cotton. "I need some time to think things over."

"Do me a favor and think things over at home. Take the time that you need," Meyerson said, and he hung up.

Cotton cleaned up the dishes with Valley, kissed her good night and headed up to bed early. As he slipped off to sleep, he could hear Miles Davis on his stereo drifting up the stairs.

CHAPTER 49

I t was in his office that Cotton did his best thinking. Maybe it was the book lined walls or the comfortable chair. This day, he had to ignore the stacks of papers waiting to be scrolled over.

Cotton heard Meyerson, but he had no intention of following his advice. He was a college professor, but it was the cop in him that was reacting now. There was no way he was going to let this go. *"You came for me, he thought, I'll come for you. But who was you?"* He didn't know anything more than he did a few days ago. He made a list of things he could do—check back through the papers Chaz's brother had sent—look through the articles that he had taken from Jillian Asbury's summer house-check with Cassandra Day to see if she remembered anything else—brace up Delaware and Scott, maybe follow them. His mind drifted back to the summer house and its contents, the books, boxes, the picture... The picture? Who was in that picture? People who were in it were being eliminated. Who was left? Dolores Davis? He decided he needed to speak with her again.

"Dr. Davis, this is Cotton Cunningham. I know we've talked before, but due to certain events that have taken place regarding people we both know, I was wondering if we could get together again?"

There was a pause on the phone. Cotton thought the

connection had been severed. He remembered her demeanor from their last conversation. But then she spoke.

"Dr. Cunningham, perhaps there are things that we need to discuss. I can be available at my home tomorrow evening. Shall we say 7:00?"

Cotton was completely taken aback.

"7:00 will be just fine. Thank you." She gave him her address and then hung up.

"He called me up and proposed a meeting. I am rethinking my philosophy of stonewalling him. I am inviting him into my home and answering any of his questions," said Dolores Davis.

"He used to be a police detective, Dolores. He's used to asking questions and twisting the topic around to trip people up," said Thornton Delaware.

"Don't worry, Thornton, I've dealt with many a political windbag in my time, people who oozed slime and twisted things around. I'll be fine. We need to get him off our trail."

"But we've done nothing wrong, Dolores. We were just witnesses to many a sordid affair. Too much drama. Those days, when we were younger, well we just got in too deep."

"And now you're paying the price for it all, I know the sad story. Let me handle this. You're not guilty of anything but rash judgement."

She ended the conversation there. But was he innocent, she asked herself? He was there that night at Jillian's. What had he seen or more to the point, what had he done?

Chapter 50

Cotton had to borrow Jen Valley's car while the insurance company haggled with him over the incident. Meyerson said he would be able to issue him a campus car in a few days. It was just a matter of paperwork.

It took a while for Cotton to find the street, but he knew by some of the houses that he was travelling in the fast lane. Huge colonials with wide roads leading up to them and magnificent lawns, no doubt attended to by lawn services, were a common sight. He drove by slowly, admiring the view, while thinking about his own humble abode.

Her house was in keeping with most of the others. It had a magnificent wrap around porch that gave the house a southern look. Indeed, it had the air of an old-time plantation, minus the slave quarters, off course. It was three stories high with yellow clapboard siding. Hanging plants and wicker furniture decorated the porch. There were rosebushes lining the driveway and three huge live oaks in the front yard. It was a house that spoke of opulence.

Davis met him at the front door.

"Come in, come in," she said with a voice full of hospitality.

He entered a foyer with a marble floor and floral arrangements. A large widening staircase bisected the floor into two sections. To the right lay a large living room with a stone fireplace as the focal point. The furniture was heavy wood and the rugs oriental. To the left lay a huge dining room with a table that could seat at least twelve. Both areas led back to a modern kitchen and sitting room that turned out to be their destination.

"Coffee or wine?" she asked.

"Coffee would be fine," said Cotton.

He was momentarily disarmed by her charm. In their past meeting she could hardly contain her distain over being interviewed about a murder. Here, she was the picture of the congenial host.

"Dr. Davis, thank you for your hospitality. I will try to make this brief."

"Don't worry. I wanted to make up for the rather curt manner that I assumed at our last meeting. Please feel free to ask any questions. I will be more forthcoming," she said.

They were seated at a small table in front of deck doors that led out to a spacious back yard. He handed her the picture that he had taken from Asbury's summer home.

"I didn't have this in my position the last time we talked. It seems that you were friends with them," he remarked.

Davis studied the picture as if it was the first time she had seen it.

"Yes, that brings back a very enjoyable lake holiday, many years ago," she said. "I'm sorry if a gave the impression that I didn't know Jillian the last time we met. I was concerned about giving you the wrong impression of a very valuable and committed member of our faculty and a dear friend. She and I go way back, probably to when she was a junior faculty member. We have served on many faculty committees and helped entertain faculty members at our respective houses. She was a grand host and we shared fund raising activities for many organizations including the Philharmonic and the Junior League. She was charitable and gave many hours of her time for these organizations."

She was pouring coffee into fine cups. Cotton always had trouble drinking out of anything so delicate.

He fumbled with the cups before speaking.

"Were you close friends with the other people in the picture," he asked.

"Some of them, more acquittances than friends. Lisbeth Scott was very young at the time this picture was taken. She was just beginning her teaching career. Again, we met at various functions, faculty meetings and committees. She was very determined to make a good impression on the senior faculty members. She was busy publishing so she could stay ahead of the tenure chase. It was very early in the game for her. Jillian, I believe at that time was up for tenure. So was the Negro in the picture. I believe his name was Powers. I forget his first name."

"Acton," said Cotton.

"Yes, Powers. He was a very opinionated man, active in some of the more radical factions around campus. He was older than Jillian and Lisbeth. I think he had taught at some other places before UB. We took him under our wing. We thought it must be lonely, being a minority on the faculty, having no one of his own kind to talk to. Unfortunately, he was involved in a tenure track competition with Jillian and there was a falling out. Jillian received the position and Powers was let go. It was quite acrimonious at the time. Jillian did have an advantage with her publications and her relations with other faculty members."

Cotton couldn't fail but to note the condescending nature of her remarks concerning Powers. The Black man obviously was looked upon on a different level than the rest.

"This picture seemed so tranquil," said Cotton. "But now, one person is dead, another missing and a third in the hospital. What did you know about Bowers?"

"Bowers was a friend of Thornton Delaware. He was a rather insecure person. Seemed to exist on the periphery of all these occasions. It seemed strange. We were all academics and he worked with his hands. He didn't talk much. When we first met, I thought he had a speech impediment. I understand that he was just shy."

"And all the violence surrounding the group?" asked Cotton.

"Jillian's death was a suicide, a tragic occurrence. She was always a perfectionist and I believe that the pressures of her job finally got to her. Whenever I contacted her about getting together, she always would speak about work that had to be done, meetings that she had to attend. I told her that she had to slow down, but she wouldn't listen. She was dedicated to her job."

"And the others," asked Cotton.

"Bowers, I have no idea. I was never close to him, but I always thought he was a tad unstable. As far as Powers goes, well I heard he changed his name, some sort of Muslim thing and that he opened a bookstore down in the ghetto. With all the drugs that are associated with those neighborhoods, it's no wonder that he ended up in the hospital."

"Have you spoken to Delaware or Scott recently about these things?"

There was a momentary pause. Perhaps she wasn't expecting the question. Cotton noticed a slight twist in the facial expression. *Was she having trouble keeping up this façade,* Cotton thought.

"I haven't spoken to either one of them, but I have no doubt that they are as mystified as I am over these incidents," said Davis.

"I know that we've gone over this before, but is there anything about Chaz Barker, the student whose body was dug up, that could help me?" asked Cotton.

She smiled. "I never had him as a student. My field is Sociology. I believe his field was Political Science?"

"Yes, it was and his faculty advisor for his thesis was Jillian Asbury," said Cotton.

"Then I would speak to others who were around at that time in Political Science. There must be a few left in the area," she said.

Cotton thanked her for her time. As she led him out through the foyer to the door, she said, "I think that Mr. Barker's death was an isolated incident. Perhaps he was into drugs and fell in with a bad crowd," she said.

"A bad crowd, my ass, Cotton thought" as he left the ritzy section of town to return to his own walk – up.

Delaware was on the phone with Davis soon after her visit from Cotton.

"Do we have something to be concerned about?" he asked.

"I don't think so," said Davis. "I changed my approach this time. I charmed him just like he was some silly politician on the take. He has nothing on us. He asked the usual questions. I gave him the usual answers. He wanted to know about Bowers. I said I had no idea. He asked about Acton. I told him, and it was the truth, that I hadn't seen Acton for years."

"What about Bowers?" asked Delaware.

"I have no idea. I know he was quite upset about Cunningham hounding him. He called me up to complain about it the day that it happened. I told him the same thing that I'm telling you. He has nothing on any of us. He probably left town."

"I heard his car is in his driveway and his personal effects still in his house. What could have happened to him?"

"I don't know Thornton, and at this point I'm not concerned," she said.

There was a pause on the line.

"I'm thinking back to Jillian's death. Did you talk to her that day?" Delaware asked.

Now Davis paused.

"I went over to her house. It was about 6:30. She had been drinking. I tried to get her calmed down. She was very upset over the Barker boy. The unearthing of his body brought back ugly memories. She didn't know how he died. Suddenly, he was gone. It certainly solved the problem of the plagiarism and her affair. She wasn't above using his material to further her career. But she was haunted by his death. None of us knew what had happened to him. I left soon after. I thought she would calm down. Obviously, she didn't."

"I went to see her later that night. I knew she was having issues with guilt.

"It must have been around 8:30. I would have gone in, but I heard voices and I lost my nerve. I should have gone up. Maybe I could have done something."

"We all could have done something, Thornton. But we didn't act in time. She ended her own life over Barker."

"I guess she did," said Delaware.

"Of course, she did, Thornton. Of course, she did," said Davis.

Scott was the next to contact Davis.

"How did it go," she asked.

"Without a hitch," Davis said.

"He knows more than we think. He's looking long and hard at that picture. He knows that we're as thick as thieves."

"I already took care of that. I let him know that we were close as a group, but we had no knowledge of Barker's disappearance. If we stick to the party line, we will have no problems. I charmed the man."

"Bowers is gone, and I heard that Acton Powers is in the hospital in a coma. What's that all about? This isn't a coincidence. Someone is working behind the scenes. Who is it? Someone knows of my relationship with Jillian. Barker knew. Hell, I walked out right in front of him one night at her office."

"Cunningham doesn't know that. You're giving him more credit that he deserves. Don't you lose control on me, Lisbeth. You're better than that."

"I'm not cracking up, Dolores. I just want to know that Cunningham is harmless."

"He's harmless unless someone caves. Don't let it be you," said Davis.

"Don't worry," Scott said. "I'm just taking precautions."

Then Scott hung up.

What did she mean by that, thought Davis.

<h1 style="text-align:center">Chapter 51</h1>

Cotton was surprised the next day by a visitor to his office. The man was small but athletic looking. He had wavy brown hair and if it weren't for the lines in his face, he would have pegged him at about in his mid-thirties. He advanced to Cotton's desk and thrust out his hand before Cotton could leave his chair.

"I'm Ned Barker, Chaz's brother. I know this is sudden and I should have called but I couldn't take it anymore. I've taken a couple weeks off from my job. I know you have more information about my brother's death. It's been all I'm thinking about since you contacted me. I can't sleep at night. I don't think you understand Dr. Cunningham, how close a family we were. My brother's disappearance killed my father and my mother after him. It ruined our family. I owe it to them and myself to find out what happened."

It all came out in such a rush that Cotton was taken aback. Finally, he motioned to a chair.

"Sit down, Mr. Barker. It seems we have a lot to talk about," Cotton said.

"Call me Ned, please," Barker said.

"Ned, all right. I don't know where to begin. There have been more things that have come up since I talked to you at last." He looked around. "I need a break from this office. I haven't had anything to eat all day. How about we move on to a more comfortable place."

Ulrich's tavern on Ellicott Street was as comfortable as it gets. A beautiful wood bar and art deco décor were a big attraction. It was an historic tavern, having been around since 1868.

"The beef on weck and the mac and cheese are favorites," said Cotton trying to make Chaz Barker's brother comfortable.

"Look, I know I haven't contacted you, but things have happened quickly and some of them have been serious and dangerous. I didn't want you involved," said Cotton.

"Nothing that could keep me away, I'm sure," said Barker.

"Now that you're here, I'll bring you up to date on everything that's happening."

"Please do and then, I'll let you in on a few things that I've found in my brother's papers."

"Your brother's papers? I thought you sent me everything?"

"I thought I did, but the I found some more of his in my father's file cabinet," Ned said. "But you go first."

Cotton sat back. He cradled a Molson Golden in his hands.

"You're aware of the fact that your brother's advisor, Jillian Asbury is dead. She was Dean Asbury when she died."

"Yes, you had passed that much onto me," said Ned.

"Since then, there have been some other incidents." He related to Ned, how an examination of Asbury's beach house had uncovered more writings, including proof that Asbury had stolen Chaz's intellectual property."

"I knew it! Chaz didn't come right out and say it, but I knew he was suspicious because of her renewed interest in his work. Before this, she skipped meetings, showed up late and then, suddenly, she was so attentive. She was planning on using his ideas."

"I believe so," said Cotton. "She published an article in a journal after your brother died entitled, "Inside Trading, Its Moral Implications.""

Ned jumped out of his chair. "That's a take-off on the title of his thesis. It's a direct rip off!"

"I think so, too. I reported it to President Meyerson, and he told me to proceed with caution."

"Proceed with caution?" said Ned. "One of his administration became dean under false pretenses. What did he have to say about that?"

Cotton could tell that Ned was extremely upset and was attracting the attention of other diners.

"Ned, right or wrong, he thinks he is protecting the integrity of the institution. He wants to find the truth in these matters, but he didn't think it was right to expose her since she was no longer alive."

Ned quieted down somewhat but was still agitated.

"Dr. Cunningham… "

"Please call me Cotton."

"Cotton, this was my brother. The stolen intellectual property might have been a cause of his death."

"I know and I'm investigating it as such," Cotton said.

"What else has happened?" demanded Ned.

"I interviewed several people that might have been involved in your brother's disappearance. When I searched Asbury's summer home, I found a picture of a group of people posing together on a beach outing. There was Asbury, a few of her friends and a Negro named Acton Powers, who at that time was a professor at UB."

"In your mind, are they suspects?"

"They're people of interest, but the interesting side of the matter is that one of them is missing and another is in the hospital in a coma."

"Who are they?" asked Ned.

"One of them named Bowers, works in the print shop at UB and is friends with two others in the picture and had been friends with Asbury, or at least an acquittance of hers. The other is currently a bookshop owner on the east side of Buffalo. His store was firebombed recently, and he ended up in the hospital."

"I assume this has all happened to those two since you've been investigating into my brother's case?" asked Ned.

"Yes, that's right and I assume that they're all connected. I was putting pressure on Bowers in the days before he disappeared. I had visited Acton Powers and shown him the picture before he was injured. And another thing, Ned..."

"Yes," he asked.

"I ended up in the hospital after the brake line to my car was cut."

Ned sat back in his chair, the Pinot Grigio untouched.

"I'm glad I took time off, Cotton. I'm going to find out what happened to my brother. I'm going to help you get to the truth."

"Ned, I don't want you getting in over your head. I used to be a cop and I'm treading lightly. You're a civilian with good intentions but no experience. The best thing for you is to go home. I promise, with the help of the police, we'll get to the bottom of this."

Ned was shaking his head. "I can't Cotton. This has

been plaguing me day and night since I've talked to you. I can't let go now."

"Ned, I can't work with you, and I can't give you any more information. I feel like I'm responsible for you being here and I don't want to get you involved any more than you are."

They left Ulrich's separately. Cotton feeling the responsibility of adding another person to the problem. He had a feeling that he would hear more from Ned in the coming days.

Chapter 52

It was a cloudy sky, and the weather dictated the somber mood both inside and out. He was still sore from the accident and couldn't sit down for any great length of time. He paced back and forth, stopping to stretch every few minutes.

Cotton was on the phone, in his office, speaking with Ted Demaris, who worked for the Buffalo Police Department. Ted worked in the motor pool and was frequently assigned to examine cars that had been involved in accidents where the threat of tampering was possible.

"Cotton, there's no doubt about it. Your accident was not due to wear and tear on your break line. That hardly ever happens, by the way. Your accident was due to the intentional cutting of your break line. We can tell because it was a clean cut."

"I thought it might be, Ted. Did you find any other signs of tampering with the automobile?"

"Nope, that was the only thing that was unusual. How are you doing, good buddy, I heard that you didn't have a soft landing."

"I'm fine Ted. Now all I have to do is fine the skunk who did this."

"Good luck to you. Sorry, I'm in a rush. I have to examine a Lincoln Continental that crashed the other day. It belonged to the mayor, but he wasn't in it when it took a nosedive."

Cotton was pretty sure that was going to be the finding, but he had to go through protocol. Now he knew it was personal.

JEN Valley suddenly appeared at Cotton's office door.

She closed the door and turned towards Cotton. She had tears in her eyes.

"Cotton, put this all aside. I can't stand it."

Cotton took her hand and sat her down.

"Jen, I can't do that. Someone's out there. A killer and that person tried to kill me."

"That's just what I'm saying, Cotton. Someone's trying to kill you. They tried once and they might try again. Cotton, we're starting a life together. I don't want it to end over something that happened twenty years ago that you had nothing to do with."

They sat for a while in silence.

Then Jen got up walked over to the door, opened it, and walked out.

Cotton sat there in silence for a long time.

Chapter 53

The next day, Cotton found Cassandra Day in the office she was granted as a professor emeritus. She wore a black turtleneck sweater, and she was loaded down with jewelry, mostly turquoise from trips to Mesa Verde. Being retired, she was able to travel whenever she wanted, and she was never without a tan. She was lounging back in a chair, reading a book by William Appleman Williams entitled *The Tragedy of American Diplomacy.*

"I find myself rereading Williams to find out where America has gone wrong." She put the book down and swiveled to face Cotton.

"I suppose that you've been following the path this case has been taking." asked Cotton as he sat down in an expensive rocker. The room was subdued but still spoke of Day's expensive touch. Paintings from the turn of the century lined the walls. A Persian rug dominated the space. A comfortable looking couch sat in front of a book lined wall. A small roll top desk stood on the opposite side.

"I've heard bits and pieces from various friends about that man Bowers disappearing and Acton Powers ending up in the hospital," she said.

Cotton told her about his automobile accident, and she looked worried.

"Cotton, I really think you should excuse yourself from this ordeal. You are a college professor. You're no longer a policeman. You are too valuable to be put in a dangerous position. This twenty-year-old affair is taking its toll on you. It's not your business, Cotton. Give it up."

She sounded genuinely concerned.

"Thank you for your concern, Cassandra, but I don't think I can ignore a threat on my life."

He went on to explain to her about Ned Barker and his sudden appearance on the scene.

"I'm worried that he's going to put himself in a dangerous position trying to find out about his brother's death."

Cotton never explained to Day about the theft of intellectual property or Ned's theory that Chaz Barker had something to hold over her head. It was a sensitive subject and one that Marty Meyerson would not like to be made public. Cassandra was a sympathetic ear and Cotton had occasionally used her as a sounding board.

"Cotton, have you ever entertained the idea that Barker was mugged by a petty criminal who was looking for cash? They didn't mean to kill him and when they found out what they had done, they panicked and buried the body."

"I never considered that, Cassandra. This has all the markings of a premeditated murder."

"Premeditated murder? Over what? A college student? In an academic setting? Have you checked into Barker's character. Was he into drugs? Gambling?

"Did he owe money to, what do you call them—the mob?"

"I've investigated his family. They're solid middle class. His father was a professor at Kenyon. There was nothing to indicate that he would run with anyone undesirable," he said.

"If he did have an association with gamblers or the

mob, maybe you're getting too close to whoever murdered him. It was twenty years ago, but the person might still be around."

Cotton thought about it. "You might be right, Cassandra. I'll have to give it more consideration."

Chapter 54

Cotton was watching the evening news. Walter Cronkite was patiently explaining the number of soldiers that had died that day in Viet Nam. He watched coffins being unloaded from military planes and being arranged solemnly on the tarmac when the phone rang.

The word was that his father was declining rapidly. He contacted his sister and proceeded to the old folk's home where he was being cared for. The parking lot was mostly empty when he pulled in.

When he made it through the front doors, a doctor and nurse were there to meet him.

"I'm sorry, Dr. Cunningham, He expired just moments ago. We 'll leave you alone with him."

Cotton, in a daze, followed them to his father's room. He was lying on his bed, partially covered by blankets. His face had a neutral expression. Cotton pulled up a chair and just sat there.

He had prepared himself for this eventuality, as much as one could. As he gazed at this man, this man who Cotton had never loved, he was surprisingly filled with guilt. Where was this guilt coming from? Guilt that he wasn't there at the end as much as he could be? Guilt that he hadn't tried to bond with him when he was younger? Was Cotton's father typical of the older generation of men, men who drank after work, came home, and demanded supper on their time, didn't help with the kids and ruled with an iron hand? Was Cotton supposed to realize that?

"Is that all you could ever be Dad? Did we expect you to be more than you could be? Were you like your father and his father before him? "

He sat there asking his father questions until his sister entered the room.

THE funeral was at Fourteen Holy Helpers Church on Indian Church Road. The pall bearers were Cotton and Fred and some of his father's friends from the steel plant. It was a simple affair. His father was not a regular attendee at church. Jen was there along with family friends from when Cotton grew up.

Cotton had not been inside a church for years and the familiar smells of incense, and wood polish brought back memories. He was surprised to see Meyerson, Drew and Cassandra Day in attendance.

The priest made a short speech, repeating information that Cotton and his sister had relayed to him. The speech was generic, remembering Cotton's father as a good provider and stalwart member of the community. It reminded Cotton why he stopped attending church.

Afterwards, there was a luncheon catered by the American Legion—Cotton was a veteran. He commiserated with people he hardly knew, and the affair left him with a feeling of emptiness and despair.

He left the luncheon after the formalities were observed and went to the nearest bar and got roaring drunk. He couldn't remember how he got home.

Chapter 55

otton got the call, right after his afternoon class.

"Cotton, this Blake Barnaby."

Blake was a Buffalo cop.

"Hey, Blake, what's. up?"

"Cotton, we've got a fellow in the lockup who claims he knows you. His name is Ned Barker. He was caught roaming around some people's yards up in Amherst last night. A neighbor called it in. He gave us your name. Said it had to do with a case you both were involved in on campus. Do you know anything about this?"

Ah, shit, Cotton thought.

"Blake, I know him. I'll be down in half hour."

Cotton didn't need this aggravation. He was overloaded to begin with. He had missed classes, cancelled dates with Jen and rearranged his schedule. Now he had to babysit Ned Barker.

On the ride down, Cotton thought about Ned. He couldn't be too hard on the guy. He lost his brother. His parents died consumed in grief. And now he was haunted by all of this.

He found Blake Barnaby seated behind a desk in processing.

"Cotton, we're charging him with trespassing, a minor offense. The bail is $200. If you post it for him, we can get him out in short order."

It took two hours, two hours that Cotton didn't have. When Ned was finally released, he was glad to see Cotton.

"Thanks, man. I really appreciate it. I can pay you back the bail as soon as I get back to the motel and get my check book."

Cotton had to drive him back to his car which was two blocks away from Thornton Delaware's house.

"What were you thinking about Ned, wandering around people's yards in the middle of the night?" asked Cotton.

"These were people connected to my brother's death and they're hiding something, "he said.

Cotton had given up Lisbeth Scott and Thornton Delaware's names when he had discussed the situation with Ned.

"How do you know that?" Cotton asked.

"They were together at each other's houses, but most recently, his house."

"So, perhaps they're lovers," Cotton said.

"But she's married," Ned said.

"Do you really think that makes any difference?"

Ned slumped in his seat. He looked defeated.

"Look, I know what you're after and I realize that sitting around doing nothing is depressing, but you can't break the law to get where you need to go," said Cotton.

That brought Ned out of his momentary funk.

"I'll do anything I can to find the answers. If you don't help me, I'll do it myself."

Even though he looked down and out, there was a glimmer of defiance, a touch of determination in his voice. He had no other job in his life than to find out the truth about his brother's death.

Cotton thought about that. Wasn't that what he was trying to do? Wasn't it worth all the death, all the threats, to find out the truth?

"I've been to the hospital. I tried to see Bhakta, but they wouldn't let me in. I can't hardly say that I was family. I found out the addresses of these people and thought if I could do nothing else, I could at least track them. It was late this morning – the lights were still on when I decided to get closer. I guess someone else was awake. They called in the cops."

"Well, at least you won't do that again," said Cotton.

Ned looked Cotton in the eye.

"You're holding out on me," Ned said.

"I told you what I know," said Cotton.

"I'm going to find out what happened to my brother, with or without your help," said Barker.

He got into his car and peeled away from the curb.

Chapter 56

Cotton promised Jen that they would go house hunting. This was informal, not a commitment to move in with each other.

"We're just checking out the market," said Jen.

They decided to investigate the southtowns. They met a real estate agent named Pam at the first site in the village of Hamburg. Pam was a bubbly slightly overweight woman with a frilly white blouse and a lime green skirt that extended to her ankles. She held a clipboard and acted very official. They drove to the first site.

He found 15 Worthington without much trouble. "A powdery blue cape cod with two bathrooms, two bedrooms and a beautiful kitchen that faces a deck on the outside. It's been recently painted," Pam said.

It's a disaster about Ned, Cotton thought. *His whole family ruined by the brother's death. Over some pages of a thesis. And all the senseless violence that's followed. Asbury's death—a suicide? I had interviewed her days before and she seemed what? First angry and then despondent? She admitted being his advisor, but that could have been easily traced. And her publications... they certainly were borrowed from Barker's research...*

"As you can see the kitchen carries the most modern appliances. A separate room off the kitchen for the washer and dryer. What a convenience that is..."

She most certainly is guilty of unprofessional conduct. But murder? Over a thesis? Of course, if she was discovered it would have ruined her career and everything she worked for. An impulse... no, it was premeditated. It had to have been planned. A 2x4? Quite a swing. What kind of shape was she in? She wasn't that large of a woman. Almost on the slight side. Could she have carried it off? And then the burying of the body? How was that worked out? Did she have an accomplice?

"And a convenient downstairs bathroom. But let me show you the living room. The grand fireplace with bookshelves on either side. You say you're teachers? There's your library. I can picture both of you, cozy on a winter's night reading in front of a roaring fire..."

And the picture. They all knew each other... And Delores Davis. How did she fit in? She was much older than all of them. Back when Barker disappeared some of them were still undergraduates. Acton Powers, a man who didn't fit into the crowd at all. He knew more than he was saying. There was anger there. He was cheated out of a position. He saw them for what they really were. A clique. Almost incestuous and perhaps violent?

"As we go up the stairs, you can see three bedrooms two on the right and one on the left that could be converted into a study, a man's room, very comfortable with a great view. The larger bedroom, the master, has a bathroom, with a built-in shower. Plenty of counter space for a woman's needs..."

Yes violent, but which one, or maybe more than one. An accomplice?

Scott was a suspect. Cool and calm and quite the looker.

She was tall and athletic. She was strong enough to swing a piece of wood and dig a grave.

Where was Bowers? How did he fit in? He could never be a ringleader. He didn't have the nerve. And where did he go? Was he dead or did he skip town?

But you don't skip town and leave everything behind.

And Bhakta in the hospital. Was he going to come out of his coma soon? He could provide some information. Was he the victim of neighborhood violence or did he know too much? If he did, I need to find out what it was

"Let's look at the backyard. As you can see, it's extensive almost a quarter of an acre. Plenty of room for a garden. There are exactly 15 maple trees, that means plenty of shade. Perfect for a hammock..."

And Ned. Was he going to become an obstacle to the investigation? There was no time to watch over him. He provided some vital information but now that he wanted to become a detective, he would be nothing but an impediment.

What about going back to Asbury's summer home. Would there be information that he had overlooked? The picture... there was something about the picture...

"'What do you think, Cotton? You haven't said a word since we got here. Cotton, Cotton, where are you?"

"Oh, Jen, ah, yes, what do you think, honey?"

"Well, I've been talking all along, Cotton. I want to know what you think?"

"What I think? Well, I think it's time for lunch, don't you?"

"Cotton, that was embarrassing. She took all that time showing us that house and you were in another world. What's wrong with you?'"

"I'm sorry, Jen. It's this whole business with the Barker murder. I can't think of anything else. There must be something I've overlooked, and I can't figure it out."

Jen looked concerned. "Cotton, I've been worried about you ever since your accident. You can't seem to focus on anything else. How are your classes going?"

"All right, I guess. I find myself drifting sometimes. Meyerson suggested a leave of absence, but I won't do that. I intend to fulfill all my obligations to my students. "

"Maybe a little weekend getaway will do you some good. Remember that trip we spoke of earlier in the year to Concord? Just what two history teachers need for a romantic getaway. A little bit of Transcendentalism. We can take the bikes and roam around the old North Bridge."

CHAPTER 57

otton agreed and the weekend found them, bikes hooked up on a rack on the back of Cotton's car, travelling down the Thruway on a Friday afternoon under overcast skies.

The scenery on the way was typical Western New York landscape. The area around Buffalo is flat. The drive was monotonous until they got part way across the state and moved into the Finger Lakes region. Small cities like Rochester, Batavia, Oswego, and Albany marked the way.

It was a straight shot on Rt.90 until you reach the Massachusetts turnpike and turn off at exit 21A. That takes you past Worcester towards Lowell.

It took a little longer than six and a half hours before they pulled into the parking lot of the Concord Inn. The Inn is the place to stay in Concord if you can afford it and if, and that's a big if, you can get reservations. Fortunately, they were able to book them at short notice.

The original structure was built in 1716 and it's still standing. It became a hotel in 1889. It's on the National Register of Historic Places and rightfully so. It's in pristine condition and is filled with colonial ambiance. The main part of the inn was used as an ammunition store during the Revolution. It has a connection with Henry Davis Thoreau. His grandfather build the eastern section of the building and Thoreau lived there for two years while he attended Harvard.

It was, in other words, the perfect place for two history buffs to stay while visiting one of the most historic towns in the United States. And the perfect place to forget about murder.

THE next day, they rose early and took breakfast at the inn, ham and eggs for Cotton and fruit for Jen. They started the day with a trip to Louisa May Alcott's Orchard House where they learned about the early life of one of America's foremost female authors.

Both Cotton and Jen had been there before – Cotton when he was a boy and Jen on a college trip with friends, but they still delighted in the information.

Next was the Old North Bridge, perhaps Concord's most famous outdoor attraction. It was obligatory to get a picture taken and they commandeered a visitor to do so.

The Old Manse was next, home at one time to both Nathaniel Hawthorne and Ralph Waldo Emerson.

Finally, before supper, they took in the Ralph Waldo Emerson House which was in excellent condition and the talk from a well-versed guide was well worth the price of admission.

They ate dinner at one of the many small coffee houses that ring the square.

"Now, isn't this just what you needed," asked Jen as they settled in with their second cup of coffee.

"No doubt about it," answered Cotton. "You know, I was a teenager when I came here with my uncle who was a history buff. As you can imagine, many of these things went right over my head. This time around, I was able to soak in much more."

"It makes you wonder how so many important thinkers could live within such a small radius," said Jen. "Thoreau, Emerson, the Alcotts, and Hawthorne to name just a few. Throw in visitors from Boston like Margaret Fuller and you have an intellectual center."

Cotton agreed. He was enjoying the weekend getaway. There were few thoughts of what was transpiring back on campus.

"What I've found out was that it wasn't just these figures that we all revere, but their family members as well. Louisa May Alcott's father, Bronson Alcott, was a pioneer in advocating new ways of teaching young children. He was also an abolitionist and advocate for woman's rights. Thoreau's sisters, Helen and Sophia were passionate abolitionists. Helen was friends with Frederick Douglass and corresponded with William Lloyd Garrison."

They spent the rest of their weekend getaway biking around Concord and enjoying the atmosphere. Cotton investigated the windows of the numerous real estate companies.

"Whew, "he said. "I thought the prices of homes in suburban Buffalo were high. These prices are out of this world."

"You've got to realize that this is a bedroom community within commuting distance of Boston and a huge tourist attraction. That's what the real estate people mean when they say, location, location location."

The trip home the next day was uneventful, but they returned revitalized having put college and mayhem behind them for a while.

Chapter 58

Cotton was sitting behind his desk in his office correcting papers about the Progressive Movement. It was one of his favorite periods in American history. He was especially fond of showing his students pictures that Jacob Riis took of the tenement houses in New York City. There were no smiles on these faces as they struggled to overcome poor ventilation, improper sanitation, and crowded rooms.

Cotton caught the phone call minutes after he settled in.

"Cotton, this is Jefferson Drew. There's a word going down that a confrontation is going to take place tonight. I thought you might want to know."

"Who's involved?"

"The veterans are marching. That's a change. And SDS has a counter demonstration on the move. I think there might be a problem."

"When and where?" asked Cotton.

"The vets' march is starting at 6:30 outside the union," said Drew.

"I'll be there," said Cotton.

THE evening was foul. There was a steady rain and a wind kicked up around the union strong enough to make a simple conversation difficult. Darkness had settled in and the lights in the windows blinking on and off on campus set an eerie tone to the proceedings. By the time the vets were assembled, most of them, without proper rain gear, were soaked.

Members of SDS, whose numbers were starting to grow, were off to the side of the Union in their traditional garb of denim jackets, jeans, and combat boots. Some wore armbands with initials proclaiming their affiliation to various groups. Others had hastily scrawled signs with various anti-war messages scribbled on them. The signs, already disintegrating from the pelting rain, would soon be discarded.

Cotton's goal was to seek out the leaders of the two groups and try to encourage them to avoid any violent overtures. He was having difficulty doing this because of the weather and the fact that he wasn't as familiar with the veterans group.

He looked around the SDS assembly until he found Reggie Gleason, one of their leaders.

Reggie was busy talking to two other students under an umbrella. Cotton had Reggie in one of his classes the previous semester. He found him to be imperious and hot tempered. He had butted heads with him more than once in class over the war in Viet Nam.

"Reggie," said Cunningham. "I hope you're not planning on disrupting the vets' march."

"And if we are, what are you going to do about it?" he asked.

Members of each group began to move closer together. Cotton could see multiple security officers placing themselves between the groups and he thought he saw a glimpse of Jefferson Drew off to the side.

"My intentions are to make sure that the groups respect each other's territory. It should be yours, too," said Cotton.

"Be careful about telling me about what I should be doing. My father tried that, and we got into it heavy. He ended up with a broken jaw," said Reggie.

Gleason was intimidating. He was a regular sight at the University gym, power lifting in the weight room. Cotton noticed that he was carrying part of a 2x4 in his left hand.

"Reggie, I don't want to see anybody getting hurt."

"Then stand aside and watch us assert our right to demonstrate."

Convinced that he was not going to be able to deter the SDS members, he turned and walked over to the vets group. He was joined by Drew and one of his security men. The leader of the vets' group was short, but stocky and wore a goatee. His name was Jamison and Cotton recognized some insignias on his green jacket.

"Jamison, we're trying to avoid any violence," said Drew. "I will keep my men close by your people to see that that doesn't happen."

Cotton introduced himself and let Jamison know that he had served in Korea and that he appreciated his service.

"We have a lawful right to march peacefully, but we are no strangers to violence. I suppose that I've seen more than most of these youngsters."

Jamison had a look in his eye that Cotton was afraid of. This was a man who was not used to backing down.

The vets' group was composed of about fifteen members, hunched over with hands in their pockets due to the rain. They marched steadily down the side of the Union and Cotton could see that they would soon come in close contact with the SDS marchers.

Cotton crossed his fingers and hoped that the weather would disperse the people before anything thing serious took place.

A few minutes later found both groups marching almost side by side and anxious looks were exchanged.

The SDS members started chanting before too long and their tirades were getting on the nerves of the veteran's group. It wasn't long before one the SDS members moved too close to the vets.

"Get out of my space, motherfucker," one of the vets said and gave the SDS member a shove.

And then all hell broke loose.

It started with some pushing and shoving with members of both groups slipping and sliding in the mud and rain. Then, one of the vets took a swing and connected. Then the lines of march disintegrated and soon there were bodies sprawled on the ground.

Gleason, who had the 2x4 in hand, approached Jamison. Cotton saw that confrontation coming and thought to himself that Gleason was going to learn a lesson the hard way. When Gleason lifted the piece of wood, Jamison sidestepped him, planted a foot beside him, grabbed the bigger man and threw him violently to the ground. Gleason stayed on the ground.

In a few minutes, security had controlled the situation by backing the groups away from each other. The confrontation had only taken a few minutes and due to the weather and the ground condition, neither of the groups had enough traction to throw any decent punches. As it turned out, no one had the stomach to continue the fray.

The only real damage done was to Gleason who ended up at the hospital with a fractured arm.

Both Cotton and Drew got together after the combatants had left, picking up broken signs and debris.

"I thought that Gleason was getting in over his head with the vets' leader," said Cotton.

"Why's that?": asked Drew.

"Did you see those patches on his jacket?" said Cotton.

"I guess. Some decals sewn in?" asked Drew.

"Yes, they were," said Cotton. "They meant the 75th Ranger Regiment. He was in an elite fighting force. He took it easy on Gleason."

"We must get these people together again to work on a compromise. We can't have this continue to happen," said Drew.

"Maybe get Meyerson involved," said Cotton.

"My problem," said Drew, "is to find out how many of these demonstrators are really enrolled at UB. I don't think that's a problem with the vets, but there were some SDS people here that I've never seen before. Some might have been high school students."

"Like they say on Eyewitness News at the end of the day. Do you know where your children are?" said Cotton.

Chapter 59

Cotton was walking across campus, wondering when the next shoe was going to fall. As he passed many of the older buildings, he wondered about the proposed plans to build a new campus in Amherst. Traditionally, UB had been a city campus, with roots dug deep. Now it wanted to move much of the institution into the suburbs. The same thing was happening with the Buffalo Bills. They wanted to build a new stadium and much of the talk centered around a move to Orchard Park, a trendy suburb. There were people who thought that a downtown stadium near the waterfront would bring the city back to its old glory. Cotton liked the old main campus. He also knew that the wheels of progress were hard to stop.

Without warning, a student caught him from behind.

"Dr. Cunningham, you're a friend of Jimmy Salukis, aren't you?"

Pat Jenson was a veteran and Jimmy's buddy. Cotton had seen them hanging around campus many times. They were often in the same classes.

"Sure, Pat. Why do you ask?"

"Well, he got into a fight last night. Two SDS students wanted him to march with them. He told them he wouldn't. He said if he marched with any group, it would be the vets and besides, he didn't want to get involved.

There were words said and I think Jimmy just lost it. He took on both and busted someone's jaw. The other one took off. Security called the cops, and they pulled Jimmy in. The student that got hurt wants to sue. All I know is that he spent the night in jail."

"OK, "said Cotton. "I've got a class now, but as soon as it's over, I'll investigate it."

Cotton cut his history class short, which never seemed to bother the students, and he walked back to his office to make a call to the police. A friend of his, Debbie Allen, took the call.

"Yeah, Cotton, he's in the lockup. He was processed last night. He decided not to take his one call last night. He made it to someone this morning. He was booked on assault. You can see him if you want. Seems like a good kid."

"He is a good kid, and I don't see why he was booked. Wasn't he provoked by two students into a fight?"

"The story we got, and this came from the two students in the fight, was that Salukis was the instigator. They said he confronted them and threw the first punch which resulted in the broken jaw."

"Were there any other witnesses?"

"None that came forward," said Allen.

"I'll be right down to talk with him," said Cotton.

"He ain't going anywhere," Allen said.

By the time Cotton got to the station, on Court Street, it was in the middle of a shift change. Cotton didn't know the officer at the front desk but setting up an appointment to see Jimmy was a simple procedure. It wasn't long until he was face to face with Salukis.

"Hey, Jimmy, I guess you faired better in this fight," said Cotton.

Salukis looked like most people who had spent the night in jail. He was unshaven, he looked groggy, and his clothes were disheveled.

"Yeah, I did, but they got it all wrong. They say I sucker punched the kid. I was ganged up on by two students who started the fight. I was defending myself."

"It didn't help you that there were no witnesses," said Cotton.

"It was in a dark corridor," said Salukis. "They picked a good place to start something. By the way, I called your number this morning. It went to the answering machine."

"I haven't been home yet," said Cotton. "What are you going to do about bail?"

"As soon as they set it, I'll be out."

"Do you have the money?" asked Cotton.

"Depends on the amount," said Salukis. "Do you know what it might be?"

"I have no idea," said Cotton.

"They think tomorrow morning. The reason I called you is that I might be a little short on cash. If the bails too high, I might not be able to make it. I was wondering if you could help?"

Cotton was thinking, *Two times in the past two weeks. What am I a bail bondsman?*

"Yeah, I can help. Is there anything that you need at home that I can bring in?'

Jimmy gave him a list of things, including some textbooks and arranged for Cotton to get a key. Cotton said he could bring them in later in the day.

"Jimmy, when you get out, we have to talk," Cotton said.

"Yeah, I know. This is a big problem. To tell you the truth, I'm thinking of dropping out. That or transferring." He sounded discouraged.

"I don't think a drastic move is in the cards yet," said Cotton. "Sit tight."

"I ain't going anywhere," he said.

Chapter 60

Cotton didn't like formal affairs, but as a special assistant to the President, he was forced to attend a few and this was one of them. It was a dinner that included top notables at the college and included the State's Regent who wanted to know what the problem was in Jillian Asbury's death. Meyerson and Cotton sat across from the Regent.

"You know, Martin, I have received phone calls from parents about Asbury's death. Nothing serious, but they read about it in the newspapers and want to know the story behind it. Are we working our deans so hard that they become suicidal? Did we hire someone who had problems to begin with? How is that issue coming?"

Meyerson, with a slight glance in Cotton's direction, replied to the Regent.

"Albert, we hire hundreds of people at a State University. We do a good job of evaluating their capabilities. Most of them work out just fine. Occasionally, some of them are overcome with the complexities of their lives. I believe that was the case with Dean Asbury. We didn't see it coming because the dean was a proud person and dedicated to her duties."

Cotton thought, *He's playing the suicide angle. That's just fine, but if it turns out to be murder, he's going to be on a hot spot. If I know Meyerson, he won't run from that. He'll want the truth to come out. He's an honest man with a diffi-cult job.* "I'll buy that, Martin. I can play up the sympathy angle, but after what happened last year, we can't afford more violence on a state campus. You were involved with that, weren't you, Cunningham?"

Cotton was trying to avoid any conversation with the Regent. No good could come of it.

"Yes, sir. I had a hand in wrapping it up."

"Wasn't Mohamad Ali involved in it? Or was he still going by Cassius Clay? I don't adhere to his politics. Black Muslim, isn't he?"

"Yes, sir. He's a Muslim."

Meyerson wisely switched the topic.

"Albert, we'll need your help when we push the proposal for that new campus in Amherst. UB needs an upgrade. We need to move into a new age. The campus in Amherst will make UB a flagship in the SUNY system."

Cotton breathed a sigh of relief. The rest of the evening went smoothly.

CHAPTER 61

Cotton was in Jefferson Drew's office early. It was cold and utilitarian. No pictures, no comfortable furniture, no clutter. Just a metal desk and matching file cabinet. No indication of anyone in his life. In fact, Cotton knew little about the head of security, except that he was a city cop before he took the campus job. If he took the campus job to get away from the grit of the city streets, he just exchanged it for the turmoil that was apparent on a large majority of city campuses all over the country. The war, racial discrimination, woman's rights, all these topics were hot spots of student discontent. As the confrontation between the vets and SDS showed, there was no time for leisure. If anything, he was under the spotlight. Cotton knew that Drew always wanted to handle problems without calling in the Buffalo Police on campus. Neither Meyerson nor Drew wanted to bring in outsiders. The Buffalo Police thought that the students were being handled with kid gloves.

The ringing of the phone broke into their conversation.

"Security office. How can I help you?" "Yes... That's right... Was their any identification on the body? I'll be right over."

Cotton could guess about the abbreviated conversation.

"Bowers?"

"It might be Bowers."

"Mind if I tag along?" asked Cotton.

Cotton deferred as much as possible when dealing with Drew. He needed to be on his right side to do his job.

"Nope, come on along. Another set of eyes is always a good idea," said Drew.

They drove in separate cars. Cotton didn't want to depend on anyone to drive him back for a class. Drew might want to stay longer or pursue another angle of the case.

They drove to a wooded area on the outskirts of the town of Clarence. Clarence was one of those areas that was quickly becoming an affluent bedroom community linked to Buffalo. Cotton and Drew ended up in a nature preserve.

They parked their cars on a gravel area adjacent to the preserve. There were multiple vehicles present, including two squad cars, the medical examiner's Volkswagen, a couple of Buffalo detectives' Crown Vics and a crime scene van.

Both Cotton and Drew knew the detective in charge.

"We don't want to disturb the crime scene any more than it's been," said Ozzie Bradford, a big, burly Black man. He was already sweating profusely even though the air was cold.

"The body was discovered by a jogger. It was off the jogging path, in the woods. He had his German Shepard. with him. The dog started barking and swerved off the path and plowed into the woods. The jogger took off after him. It was his practice to let the animal off the leash on the path because he hardly ever met anyone out here. The dog stopped and started pawing at an area of ground that showed that it had been recently disturbed. The man discovered some personal articles, and it soon became apparent that something was buried there. He called the police and a full-scale investigation followed. We discovered a body that had been in the ground for approximately two to three weeks. There were no articles of identification on him, but we were aware of a man who supposedly was missing who worked at the University of Buffalo. That's when the police notified you and asked you to come down and verify the identity."

"No problem," said Drew. "I 've brought along Cotton Cunningham, who has been asked by President Meyerson, as his representative, to investigate the matter."

Cotton and Drew moved through a thick patch of ground cover until they came to a clearing. Multiple people were surrounding the body, many of them at a safe distance. Cotton and Drew proceeded to the body which was being looked at by the medical examiner. Cotton knew old Dr. Creech who had been the medical examiner on and off for over twenty years. Creech gave a grunt of recognition to Cotton and moved aside when asked by Bradford.

The body was face up and all tangled with dirt and mud. The hair was matted down, and the face was bruised. The eyes were closed but the lips were curled back to show an array of yellow teeth. The identification was easy. It was Paul Bowers.

CUNNINGHAM, Bradford and Drew were situated in Bradford's office at Police Headquarters. It was small, utilitarian, and colorless. Standard gun metal desk and file cabinets filled the office. Pictures of family and also a small dog were aligned to the side.

"I need you to tell me all you know about Bowers. Don't leave out anything," said Bradford his feet up on a desk drawer. He had a pack of Lucky Strikes out, but he hadn't lit up yet.

Cotton was facing a difficult situation. He could reveal everything all the way back to Chaz Barker's death, twenty years ago or he could give Bradford an abbreviated version starting with Asbury's supposed suicide. Or he could leave it up to Jefferson Drew. He chose to let Drew do the talking.

Drew had calm way of delivering information that made it understandable and the listener comfortable. There was a slight Southern pitch to his voice that would have made him an excellent storyteller if the information weren't so morbid.

"The campus investigation began with the discovery of a body identified as Chaz Barker, a student who disappeared in the late forties. Paul Bowers was a person of interest who was part of a group of people that we were talking to because of the suicide/death of Dean Jillian Asbury. Asbury was Barker's mentor on his PhD thesis. Cotton spoke to Bowers more than once and Bowers seemed agitated over the investigation. He then disappeared. This death is suspicious as it's tied to both the deaths of Asbury and Barker."

"I have to look into the paperwork on Asbury's death," said Bradford. "In the meantime, we will be speaking to all Bowers' associates. We will need help with that from you. I want his friends at work and those people who you've just mentioned. Where did he work?

"He worked at the college printshop," said Cotton.

"Those clothes that he had on are work apparel. There's ink on them."

"That means that he was approached by the murderer soon after he arrived home. He didn't have time to change his things. We know when the first day he was absent from work. That means we can say approximately when he was killed," said Bradford.

"Or abducted and killed later," said Cotton.

"You said he was upset with Cunningham's visits. What kind of person was he otherwise?" asked Bradford.

Drew looked over at Cotton.

"From what I could gather, he was introverted, had few friends and mostly kept to himself," said Cotton.

"What about these other people you referred to?" asked Bradford. "Who were they?"

"They were both college professors who knew Asbury," said Cotton.

"Did Bowers hang out with these other people who knew Asbury?" asked Bradford. "A print shop worker and two college teachers, not likely associates, don't you think? How did you know they were friends?"

Cotton paused. "I found a picture at Asbury's summer home in Canada. They were all in it. They were all friends at some time or another."

Bradford stared at them. "This is way too complicated for me to digest here. I need you to make statements concerning this death and how it relates to previous investigations."

Both Cotton and Drew did that.

They both stood outside their parked cars and reviewed what had happened.

"Meyerson is going to be plenty upset over all this,"

said Drew. "It goes against his theory of suicide with Asbury."

"Asbury could have committed suicide," said Cotton. "But it wouldn't have been an isolated instance brought on by pressures from the job. What will upset Meyerson is that her death, and Barker's, are connected. The college is not going to look pretty after this is all solved."

"If it is all solved," said Drew. "Maybe Bowers is the end of the chain."

"Maybe, I have to shake the chain, a little," said Cotton.

Chapter 62

Cotton sat at the edge of Ahmed Bhakta's hospital bed at Buffalo General. The ward smelled like disinfectant, soiled sheets, and despair. He had come to ask Bhakta some questions even though he was still in a coma. He needed information, information only Bhakta could provide.

The room was small with a bathroom, bed table and two chairs. The sun was setting, but you wouldn't have known it if not for the slight reflection on the wall outside the window. The sheets on his bed reached up to his chin. Tubes and other lines were snaking in and out and the machines sounded like a morbid chorus.

"You know more than you told me, Ahmed. Or is it Acton Powers? You needed to change your whole life when you left the University, didn't you?"

Bhakta's face showed no emotion. It held lines and crevices that were stained red from the results of the fire. There was pain there beneath his repose. His eyebrows were singed and the afro haircut he had once worn was matted and white.

"What were they really like and why did you hang with them? What attracted you to them? And what caused the break? Was it really the tenure question or did you sense something else about these people, something soiled? Something that didn't smell right?"

A nurse came in to measure his vitals. There was no sign of life other that what the machines could measure. She left without a word.

'Was your life after you split from them better? You lost your job, and all those years of school and work were washed down the drain. Where could you go and what could you do?"

Cotton knew that Powers had wandered without work. He knew that he was homeless until a menial job gave him his life back and finally afforded him the opportunity to purchase his bookstore.

"Why was your store bombed? What was so important? What did you know that made you a threat?"

Cotton sat there in the silence of the room and stared at a body that couldn't answer.

CHAPTER 63

Janice Asbury was in town to finalize the sale of both houses that Jillian Asbury owned. She wanted to meet with Cotton to get an update on the investigation of her sister's death. He set a meeting with her in his office the next day. In the meantime, He had papers to correct and classes to teach.

Cotton was already to start a discussion on the Constitution when a shy student who had never raised her hand before interrupted his talk.

"Dr. Cunningham, I'm sorry to interrupt your lecture, but there are some of us in this class that are worried about the violence that we've seen lately. How safe are we? I was walking to class the other day and almost got caught in the middle of that riot between the vets and the SDS. I'm asking you because you were there and seemed to be trying to calm people down."

Cotton quickly checked his seating chart. It was a large class.

"Tonia, I don't mind changing the script in my class. It's true that there has been violence. There are different factions on campus that believe strongly in their cause. I think the vets just want to be left alone. SDS has a very heavy political agenda and we're working with them to quit being so heavy handed in their tactics."

Another hand shot up.

"I've been stopped in hallways and on campus to join in student protests. I have my own beliefs and I don't want to be intimidated into joining a cause."

Someone shouted out from the back of the class.

"This college has been in cahoots with the military and Project Themis is at the center of this. We think the college needs to take a stand on the war and on discrimination!"

Another student rose from their seat.

"I came here for an education, not to be involved in a war on campus!"

Cotton just let it roll. Students wanted to get their feelings out and they certainly did.

<h1 style="text-align:center">Chapter 64</h1>

Janice Asbury was sitting in one of Cotton's office chairs. She was dressed prim and proper as one would expect from a person who was meeting with lawyers, real estate people and prospective buyers. She had taken time out to find out where Cotton was regarding her sister's death.

"Do you have any evidence that would indicate Jillian's death was anything but a suicide?" she asked.

"The college has taken the position that it was a suicide," said Cotton, avoiding the mention of any other entanglements.

"That's not what I asked," she said.

"I know that you want more information about other aspects of the case. Since the college has taken this position and I work for Meyerson, I've been asked to discontinue any further investigations," said Cotton.

"But, you haven't?" she said.

"I haven't," he replied.

"So, where do we stand?" she asked.

"A person who was associated at one time with your sister was found dead, just recently and another person who knew your sister is in a coma at Buffalo General Hospital as the result of a bombing."

She sat up quickly.

"Tell me more about these people," she asked.

Cotton paused to collect his thoughts.

"When I searched your sister's summer home, I found a picture of a group of people. It looked like a nice day at the beach. There was your sister, Jillian, two of her fellow teachers in the Political Science department, Lisbeth Scott and Thornton Delaware, another teacher who was older, Dolores Davis from Sociology, Paul Bowers whose body was recently discovered and a Black man whose name was Acton Powers when the picture was taken, He's now known as Ahmed Bhakta."

"When was the picture taken?" asked Janice.

"I would guess 15-20 years ago, but it could have been sooner. I can only guess because I know what these people look like now and they looked considerably younger in the picture."

"And you think the origin of these present-day incidents began with the death of a student that Jillian knew?" she asked.

"It's a possibility. The more people who end up dead or in the hospital, the more I must believe so," said Cotton.

There was a knock on the door and then an exclamation.

"Oh, I'm sorry to interrupt," said Ned Barker.

"Come on in," said Cotton.

Ned came in and stood by an empty chair, not wanting to be in the way.

"Ned, this is Janice Asbury, Dean Asbury's sister. She's come to town to settle her estate."

They shook hands cautiously, aware of their sibling's connections to a very delicate situation. Cotton was starting to realize that this meeting was getting too large for his office. He, also, didn't want their conversations drifting out into hallways where gossip was prone to spread.

"I propose we carry on this conversation in a more convenient place. Lunch is on me."

They retired to Shakey's on Niagara Falls Blvd, north of Sheridan. It had piano and banjo nightly and great pizza. They got a corner booth.

Ned started in, even before the waitress got to the table.

"Your sister was my brother's thesis advisor," he said.

"That's what Dr. Cunningham has told me, but don't look to me for much information. My sister and I were estranged for much of our adult life."

"Dr. Cunningham has revealed to me that your sister might have been stealing my brother's ideas. He said that some of her work after my brother died had elements of his work, that it could have been stolen intellectual property."

Janice Asbury stared at Barker.

"I never had a good opinion of my sister, Mr. Barker. We had our differences. But I know nothing about her behavior after she left our hometown."

"My brother's death destroyed my family. My father died, completely absorbed in finding out what happened to my brother. My mother died soon after. I was content with my life until Dr. Cunningham called with information about your sister. Then I became, like my father, completely absorbed in the situation."

"Mr. Barker, I'm sorry that your life has been so upset over your brother's death. I hope my sister was not involved, but I can't assure you of anything. I'm just here to settle her affairs as quickly as possible."

The mood was so solemn that it didn't seem like the

time for food. They ordered drinks and continued in silence.

After a while, Janice Asbury excused herself for a meeting with a perspective buyer.

Barker and Cotton remained at the table.

"I haven't been sitting around, you know," said Barker. I've been at the college talking to people. I've even had your security chief on my tail."

Cotton imagined Jefferson Drew wouldn't take kindly to an outsider prowling around campus asking questions.

"I found a lead." he said.

Cotton, surprised, asked, "What kind of lead?"

"I spoke with the custodian on the floor where you work. Custodians see and overhear more than you think. It's what his father saw and heard that interested me."

Now Cotton was totally confused.

"What do you mean, his father?" asked Cotton.

"His father was a custodian also. Back in the 1940s. He remembers what happened with my brother. And he was privy to a lot of interesting things that happened around the Political Science department back then—rumors and such."

"What kind of rumors?" Cotton asked.

"His son wouldn't go into it. He called it gossip. But I pressed him on it. I got the phone number of his father. He's been retired for many years. Lives off his pension in a little flat on Bailey Avenue. He said he'd talk to me if I didn't mind buying him a few brews after hours. I agreed to that and he's going to meet me tonight at Mulligan's bar, wherever that is. You're welcome to come along."

Chapter 65

The meeting was arranged, and Cotton was there at the appointed time.

Mulligan's Brick Bar was not the Ritz, but it was much loved by its patrons. Cotton found a parking place—no mean feat in Allentown on a Friday night. They met the retired custodian in question, a Mr. Joseph Dailey, who had settled in comfortably at the bar. Introductions were made and they retired to a side table upstairs, away from the noise and distractions.

Dailey was a small man, with a mustache that reminded Cotton of Adolph Hitler. He was thin, almost emaciated, but proved through the evening that he was capable of handling prodigious quantities of ale without slurring a word. They spoke of his son for a few minutes before getting down to the topic at hand.

He assured Ned Barker that he remembered his brother's disappearance well.

"It was the talk of the campus for weeks on end. Everyone was getting interviewed, from the top people all the way down to the peons like me. Plenty of students, too."

"Do you remember whether anyone had ideas about what had happened to him?" asked Ned.

"Lots of ideas—jealous girlfriends, drugs, and such. A lot of rumors floating around."

"My brother was never involved with drugs, I can tell you that," said Ned, who was quite upset at the suggestion.

"I wasn't saying he was, buddy, just that that was the gossip of the campus."

Cotton interrupted. "What was it like working in those departments back then?"

Dailey laughed. "I wouldn't have told anybody at the time, but there was quite a bit going on back them and not just among the students."

"What do you mean?" asked Ned.

"Faculty with faculty and sometimes faculty with students. I saw a lot," said Daley.

"Got any names?" asked Cotton.

"I'm having a hard time remembering, but a few more brews could refresh my memory."

They ordered another round and Dailey continued with his story.

"I remember some of the professors, even their names. About the same time that boy disappeared."

"That boy was my brother," said Ned quietly.

"Well, I remember one night. You see I usually work during the day, but this time I was working an extra shift because Ed Jenson was sick. I was sweeping up in the Political Science department and I see a student go into Asbury's office. Now, at that time, Asbury was a young one and I swear there wasn't much of an age difference."

"An age difference between who?" asked Cotton.

"Well, between Asbury and the student that went into her office. Now usually, when students visited their professors, the doors were wide open. But not always. And I tell you the noises I heard made me embarrassed. And then there was the guy with the limp."

"With a limp?" said Cotton.

"He was part of it too. It was a parade. And there was an older one also. But she was more of a listener, didn't go in at all. She got her kicks on the outside of the door."

Cotton thought *Dolores Davis.*

They went on through more beers before it was hard to tell the truth from fiction because of the rambling nature of the stories. Dailey was just about passed out, and Cotton had to call a cab to get him home.

"How much of that do we believe? "said Ned.

"I have to sort it all out," said Cotton as he left Baxter outside the bar.

Cotton was speeding towards the hospital. Construction slowed him down and he cursed as he took a detour on side streets of neat residential housing interspersed with projects being built for low-income residents.

He had gotten the word that Bhakta had finally come out of his coma.

He rushed through the doors, identified himself, got an ID badge and made his way to Bhakta's room on the third floor.

He wasn't the only person there. Some of his friends from the bookstore were hanging back, waiting for a doctor to come with more news of his condition.

Bhakta was sitting up in bed, in much better shape than he had been in Cotton's previous visit.

"Do you remember me?" said Cotton.

Bhakta gazed at Cotton for a moment and then replied.

"Yeah, you came and visited me about my old college

days. You had that picture of all those people. The picture that was taken at the beach. You asked all those questions."

"Yes", said Cotton. "And I have one more important question to ask you."

Chapter 66

Cotton paused in Cassandra Day's driveway. He was still mulling over what he was going to say and how he would proceed. He finally got out of the car and quietly closed the door. He had known Cassandra Day since he was a graduate student. To look at her from a different perspective was disheartening. He reached for the doorbell, but the door opened before he could ring.

Cassandra Day always seemed to be dressed to the hilt. This time she wore bell bottoms with an exotic far Eastern flair. Her sandals were lined with pearls. Her blouse was sleeveless orange with butterflies emblazoned on it. Her hair was pulled back by black clips and her red lipstick stood out on her tanned face.

"Come in, Cotton. You're always welcome in my house."

Said the spider to the fly.

They settled into the kitchen. There was a separate section with a small sofa and coffee table set apart from the cooking area.

"Yes, I've always been welcome in your home, and I've treasured our friendship. That's why I have come here tonight. I have some questions that I need to ask you and I hope the answers will ease my mind."

She smiled. "Go ahead and ask your questions."

"I visited Bhakta in the hospital tonight."

"I hope he's all right, Cotton. I was thinking of visiting him myself."

I bet you were, he thought. *That's why I requested a police presence outside his door.*

"I showed him the picture that I found at Jillian Asbury's summer cottage at Crystal Beach. You know the one that I showed you? The one that you were so helpful in identifying the people."

Cassandra didn't say a word. She just smiled.

"The only person you didn't identify was yourself. You were the person who took the picture. You were friends with that group."

"Is that such a surprise, Cotton? We were all faculty members. We had offices just down the hall from each other."

"You said you never met Bowers before, yet you were at a get-together where he was present."

Again, the smile, a smile that could hide many different things.

"All right, that was just one thing," said Cotton." But what about your husband?"

That set Day back in her chair. "What about my husband?"

"Those days in New York City, at Columbia. Those days were exciting, weren't they? Exciting and violent."

"They were intoxicating, Cotton. I was introduced to many new ideas, ideas that spurred me on to action. My husband was my guide. He was Russian, by the way. Did you know that? Changed his name to sound more American. But he kept the ideas from his mother country. He immigrated to New York in 1918. The Palmer Raids started at the beginning of 1920. Over three thousand people were arrested. Some were totally innocent. They never had any connection to the Red Menace. Of course, my husband was thoroughly Americanized at that point and escaped detection. He was already on the way to getting his appointment in the History department at Columbia. On the side, he was active with the Communist Party. But what does this have to do with me, Cotton?"

"Just a little background, Cassandra. And then I talked to a janitor."

"A janitor?" Cassandra looked completely surprised.

"Yes," said Cotton. "A janitor from back in the late 1940s. He was stationed in the history department back then. He remembers you."

Again, surprise registered on her face.

"I bet he does, Cotton. I taught in the history department. He probably saw me every day."

"Every day, Cassandra, and some nights. You see he used to work double shifts when someone was out sick. He remembers Jillian and students that used to visit her at odd hours of the day in her office, with the door closed."

Now, the smile was removed.

"He remembers you, Cassandra. Of course, you were younger then. But he gave me a precise description and it had to have been you. He said that you were around Jillian's office quite a bit. Sometimes you were listening in on student/ teacher conferences. Conferences that weren't about academics. He remembers you visiting her quite often. And again, the sounds were not what one would associate with stimulating conversation in Political Science."

"You can stop right there, Cotton. I was hoping that

what you were coming here about tonight was innocent. I regret that it wasn't. I'm afraid that you've told me too much and I must do something about it."

Cotton expected this. He fingered his old service revolver in his pocket.

"I don't think you can do much about it, Cassandra. I think you need to come down to the police department with me and you should be thinking about a lawyer."

"I don't think I will, Cotton. What do you think I should do, Thornton?"

Cotton turned around to see Thornton Delaware in the kitchen doorway holding his own revolver.

It was then that he felt a pain on the side of his head, and everything went blank.

WHEN he woke up, he was trussed up in a chair. Delaware was there with his gun and Cassandra was leaning on a five iron.

"You didn't notice my golf clubs in the corner, I still have the swing, don't I? And when I saw you waiting in my driveway, I thought a call to Thornton was in order."

Thornton Delaware was nervously fingering his revolver.

"You might have noticed when you interviewed Dr. Delaware in his office and saw the pictures on his wall, that some of them involved big game hunting. Thornton knows his guns. And his muscle comes in handy when burying bodies is involved."

Cotton was very sore and somewhat nauseous. He was conscious enough, however, to understand the implications of what Day was referring to.

"You're speaking of Barker and Bowers, I suppose," said Cotton.

Keep them talking, Cotton. Buy yourself some time. Throwing up would probably do that also.

"Thornton, I think we need to consider how to get rid of Cotton. I could use my clubs but that would create quite a mess, What about a bullet to the head?"

Delaware moved closer to get a good shot.

Cotton was passing out, but he couldn't mistake the next sounds. Doors breaking down and the sound of many feet and voices. After a while, there was the sound of wrists being cuffed. And he couldn't mistake the next sound. It was the sound of a hand slapping a face. Then he heard the voice of Joyce Asbury.

"She might have been a bitch, but she was my bitch!"

Chapter 67

They all met in Martin Meyerson's office a few days after the incident at Cassandra Day's house. There was Cotton, Jefferson Drew, Ned Barker, Joyce Asbury and, of course, a disillusioned Meyerson.

"Now that this has gotten out, I'm going to spend the next few months explaining to alumni and parents what the hell was going on, not only twenty years ago, but in the last few months. A distinguished professor emeritus, a dean, a well published professor, and Bowers. How could we hire such people? And what the hell was going on back in the post war years? And by the way, Lisbeth Scott is all lawyered up and we don't know how Dolores Davis was involved."

Cotton began. "I'll tell you everything I found out, but there are still some things that will probably never be able to be explained. But first, I would like to thank Ned Barker and Joyce Asbury. At the beginning, I thought they were just getting in the way of the investigation, but if it wasn't for their determination, I wouldn't be here. They can explain better than I can."

Ned Barker took center stage. "Cotton was feeding us information, but there were some things that he kept close to his vest. In the meantime, I was collaborating with Joyce in trying to find out more about her sister."

"We found out that we make a pretty good team," said Joyce beaming.

"We decided that the best way to find out what was going on was to follow Cotton around, "said Ned. "Joyce and I took turns. We were with him when he visited Bhakta in the hospital, and we followed him from there. We were watching from another street when Delaware showed up. It looked like something was going to break so we took a chance by edging up to the windows. When things started to heat up, Joyce hustled over to an all-night drug store and made the call to get the cops over quickly."

"And just quick enough,'" said Cotton.

"I never ran so fast in all my life," said Joyce proudly.

"All right," said Drew. "We know how you rescued Cotton, but Cotton, how did you know it was Cassandra Day?"

"She was playing me all along, getting information and I was unaware because of the respect I had for her. She was my mentor through my graduate years. I never expected her involvement until the end. It wasn't until we met Dailey, the custodian from back in the mid-forties that I realized her involvement. He described her to me, but I didn't let on to Ned or Joyce that I knew the person he was describing. And then Bhakta talked about the picture. I never thought about asking the big question – who took the picture. It was Cassandra Day.

"We weren't there in the hospital room to listen in. All we could do was follow him," said Joyce.

"After the talk with Dailey, I did some research," said Cotton. "I had to go way back to the twenties to find out about Cassandra and her husband. They were members of the Communist party in the United States. Her husband took part in many suspicious activities while a professor at Columbia. Some of those involved bombings. Their involvement was never proven, but I guessed that Cassandra might have learned about bomb making from her anarchist husband. Something that might prove to be handy twenty years later when she had to silence Bhakta."

"Then it was her that put him in the hospital," said Drew.

"That's the way I read it," said Cotton. "And after I found out that she took the picture, I thought that it was time to confront her. I really wished it wasn't her."

"But what went on twenty years ago with Day?" asked Meyerson.

"This is only guess work on my part, but we knew through Dailey that Day was hanging around Jillian Asbury, watching her every move. I think she was infatuated with Jillian and was hoping for a relationship. She saw that Jillian was entangled with Lisbeth Scott. She also heard that Jillian was using Chaz Barker and that Barker was threatening to expose her. She went to Asbury and told her that she could make all her problems go away. When news about Barker's disappearance became the talk of the campus, Asbury realized what had happened and carried around that guilt her whole life."

"So, Day killed Barker?" asked Meyerson.

"Cassandra always had a great golf swing. It didn't take too much to transfer that swing to a 2x4," said Cotton.

"But what about Delaware?" asked Drew. "I thought he was involved with Scott."

"They let me speak with Delaware yesterday. Cassandra wasn't admitting anything, but Delaware told me that he was always infatuated with Day. A glamorous professor with outstanding credentials paying attention to a student. It was intoxicating for him. And she needed another person to do the heavy lifting."

"But what about Dolores Davis?" asked Meyerson. "She's threatening to sue the college for what she says is slander in involving her in this mess."

"I'm not sure about her involvement, but I think she must have known about some of what was going on. I think she wondered about the others and their involvement. I'm not sure she realized Day's involvement. "

"And who killed Asbury?" asked Ned Barker.

"I think it was Day." said Cotton. "Asbury was threatening to break. Day couldn't take the chance. Same with Bowers. He was a loose cannon. He had to be eliminated."

"It seems like there's so much we don't know," said Joyce Asbury.

"And if Day gets a sleek lawyer, she might be able to wiggle out of some of this. Or at least deal with the prosecutor, "said Ned.

"Lets' hope not," said Cotton. "I wouldn't want someone like Cassandra Day getting out of jail."

That thought made for a somber atmosphere.

"At least, I got to know what happened to my brother," said Ned Barker.

"And my sister," said Joyce Asbury. "Even though she probably got what she deserved."

"None of this is going to end well," said Meyerson. "The college's reputation is besmirched and it's going to take a long time to change that."

"We found the truth," said Cotton. "That's got to be worth something."

"Sometimes the truth leaves a stain," said Drew. " A stain that doesn't wash away."

www.ingramcontent.com/pod-product-compliance
Lightning Source LLC
Chambersburg PA
CBHW061301210726
48293CB00003B/1056